About the author

Vincent Cristaldi was born just outside of Northern Philadelphia. Growing up, he had a vast imagination and a love of storytelling. In fact, it was his sixth-grade English teacher who first suggested that he nurture and utilize this gift. Spending a period of his life as a traveling actor, he has learned plenty about the human experience and how to set a scene. Along with his talent for acting, Vincent is also a self-trained pianist and songwriter which further fosters his passion for creativity and self-expression.

With his vast imagination he refuses to be confined to one literary genre, so let's see where he takes us next…

BROTHERS

VINCENT CRISTALDI

BROTHERS

Vanguard Press

VANGUARD PAPERBACK

© Copyright 2022
Vincent Cristaldi

The right of Vincent Cristaldi to be identified as author of
this work has been asserted by him in accordance with the
Copyright, Designs and Patents Act 1988.

All Rights Reserved

No reproduction, copy or transmission of this publication
may be made without written permission.
No paragraph of this publication may be reproduced,
copied or transmitted save with the written permission of the
publisher, or in accordance with the provisions
of the Copyright Act 1956 (as amended).

Any person who commits any unauthorised act in relation to
this publication may be liable to criminal
prosecution and civil claims for damages.

A CIP catalogue record for this title is
available from the British Library.

ISBN 978 1 80016 238 9

*Vanguard Press is an imprint of
Pegasus Elliot MacKenzie Publishers Ltd.*
www.pegasuspublishers.com

First Published in 2022

**Vanguard Press
Sheraton House Castle Park
Cambridge England**

Printed & Bound in Great Britain

Dedication

I dedicate this book to my parents Raymond and Thelma, my wife Rachel and my children Vincent James and Seraphina Loren Cristaldi.

Acknowledgements

Special thanks to Seraphinetra Artists

Rachel Asheade: Photography

Of all the days from the first of the year until now, today was by far the nicest. Spring was in the air and life was all around. The once barren branches that flailed in the breeze were starting to bud and bear the beginnings of new leaves. All sorts of creatures were about. Blue jays and robins were flying from one tree to another as they sang their praise to the coming spring. Butterflies and moths fluttered through the newly budding brush. The sun gleaned over this serene and peaceful atmosphere. Then, out of nowhere, an unnatural cracking sound echoed through the wooded area. A grazing fawn twitched an ear as she lifted her head. A few minutes later, a similar crack echoed as it broke through the serenity. Less than a quarter of a mile away there was a fair clearing. Within this clearing was a small, yet homely, wood clapboard house with a cedar shake roof. Misty gray plumes of smoke billowed from the chimney of this one-story house. The house was well maintained and well built. The front porch was decorated with two wooden rocking chairs made from an old oak tree that had fallen a few years prior. Between them was a small table of similar wood. The windows were clear with beautiful, handmade curtains that adorned the inside. The grass was neatly kept and vibrant green with nature's beauty added to it. Around the side of the house, voices could be heard. And when they were silent, again, another loud cracking sound shattered the air. By now it could be identified as the discharge of a bullet from a gun.

"Good. Very good." This praise came from John Harper who was standing beside two young boys. He was not much past fifty years of age and his hair was short and deep brown with eyes to match. John was tall in stature and athletic in build. His face bore the signs of a life hard-lived. Countless stories could be told by the wrinkles on his face.

About twenty-two years ago, he had led a different life. At that time, John used to run with the Three Brothers Gang. The gang, originally just that, three brothers, expanded to about ten members and John was one of those ten. They were noted for their uncanny ability to rob trains and banks quickly and efficiently. This was a skill that John had cultivated and brought to the gang. He had a knack for planning things out. It was almost as if he could see the whole plan and its contingencies in his mind before the first step was even taken. The life of an outlaw was definitely not easy. The more popularity you gain, the more people want to take a shot at you. And then there was the law. Sometimes you could barely sleep for an hour before you would have to be up and ride again. However, John was not like the usual outlaw. Even though he was extremely quick on the draw, he never killed anyone unless it was necessary. And the money he gained was never squandered on frivolous activities. He was saving the money in case he ever managed to live long enough to get away from this lifestyle. The whole reason he got into the lifestyle was so that one day he could live a good life. You see, his family was very poor and barely had money to put food on the table. When he was young, he had to learn to fend for himself and find ways to provide for his family. There was no amount of decent work at the time and so he resorted to stealing bread and other types of food to feed the family. When he turned twenty-two, he met up with one of the three brothers that formed the gang. They were just a budding group of vigilantes at this time, and they were interested in anyone who could wield a gun. When Johnathon explained his reasons for wanting to join, they initially accepted it and told him that was fine. And so it went on for a time where Johnathon was planning the robberies and did his best to minimize any unnecessary deaths. Most times he was successful, but sometimes things did not go quite according to plan. And in those unfortunate times, innocent people lost their lives. Although he would not show it to the others, this was a part of the life that really bothered him. After a few years of the robberies and pillaging, something happened that pushed him closer to his retiring from the gang much sooner. In a quaint small town where the Three Brothers Gang held up for a few days in hiding, he met Anna. She was a woman who, in his eyes, was the most beautiful creature ever created. And in that brief time, the two of them fell in love. And when he left, he would write her constantly. And when time permitted, he would ride off alone and visit her. And on one of these visits, his entire world changed. Anna became pregnant. As the series of events progressed, Johnathon had reached a point that he could leave the gang. The brothers were not thrilled about this because, even though they agreed with him at the start of it all, they never believed that he was serious about it. And he received opposition and resistance when he confronted them about leaving. But they finally relented and let him leave. Johnathon made it a point to not let anyone know where he was going. He bought some land in the middle of nowhere and built a small house. He had enough money set aside for them to sustain a life together. And it was a good thing for him that he left the gang when he did because it was only a few short months later that the gang was ambushed by a posse sent from the governor. The two brothers who managed to escape swore that they would exact revenge on the one they thought had betrayed them by meeting with the governor and gaining pardon: John Harper. This was untrue as John wanted nothing more in any way to do with them or that life.

He was speaking to his eldest son, Eric. Now, Eric was only eleven, but he was already skilled at the draw and the shot. He too, like his father, had short hair. It was lighter than his father's, with hints of waviness to it. His arm was still outstretched with a pistol at the other end. A small wisp of smoke billowed from the barrel as if to be a sigh of relief after the violent reaction within its bowels just a moment earlier.

"You saw the target, focused and never hesitated," John continued. "Very good. James, your turn."

James was the younger of the two siblings. He was only seven and resembled his mother. His gentle face was one of grace and innocence and the look in his eyes was as if he could, nor would, ever do wrong. A moment of silence fell as James prepared himself. Then, as quickly as he could, and not bad for a young boy of seven, he raised his arm and squeezed the trigger. The recoil jolted his arm causing it not to remain steady. His shot skimmed the side of the target. James, in a fleet of disappointment, spoke up.

"Why can't I hit the target?"

Both his father and older brother looked at him. They knew of his desire to be good at this and the frustration he felt at his continued failure.

"You'll get it, son," John reassured him.

"Don't feel bad, Jimmy. It took me a while to get it also."

Eric's words seemed to be more of a comfort to James than his father's. This was probably because, although he greatly admired his father, his admiration for his brother was greater.

"What am I doing wrong?" James asked.

"You are rushing the shot, son."

"But I have to be fast, Daddy."

"Not right now you don't. Take your time and practice the technique. When you are ready, the speed will be there."

"Show me again Daddy," James pleaded with loving eyes, "show me again."

With a mild sigh and a slight smile of approval from the side of his mouth, John asked him to pick a branch on a tree. James let his eyes scan the perimeter and dart from tree to tree. Finally, his eyes settled on one.

"That one there," he responded as he pointed to the branch that caught his eye, "near the top."

"That one?" John confirmed, pointing as well. "Okay."

He pulled out each pistol from its holster and loaded them. The two pistols he loaded had remarkable hand-carved inlaid ivory handles. The design was that of a wolf's head. The handles housed an even more ornate and beautiful chamber and barrel. It was a stunning, shining silver in color with vine-like markings on either side. Besides his family, these two firearms were his pride and joy and he diligently cared for them. Once the two gorgeous pistols were loaded, they were returned to their home within his belt. John stared at his target and then closed his eyes for a moment. He drew in a deep breath. As he exhaled, his eyes slowly opened. Then, with lightning-fast speed, he drew the pistol on his right. The first shot severed the branch, and the remaining five shots kept the branch in the air. When the first pistol was spent, it was returned to its side of the holster. And almost as fast, the left pistol was drawn. Those six shots also nailed the falling branch. A few seconds after the second pistol had expelled its last resident, the helpless remnants of the branch fell to the earth. Eric and James stared in amazement. Although they had seen this before, each time their reaction was as if it was the first time. The moment was interrupted by their mother, Anna, calling them for supper.

"We'll pick this up another day. Go on boys."

"Race you!" James challenged his older brother as he started to sprint toward the front porch. Eric ran after him.

"He's gaining on 'im. He's gaining on 'im." Eric called out as he got closer to his brother.

"Not this time!" James hollered back. But Eric pulled ahead and reached the porch first.

"I win!" Eric proclaimed.

"No fair, your legs are longer." They wrapped an arm around each other as best friends do and went inside. After supper, Eric and James and their mother were reading from the Bible as she believed the values therein would help enrich their lives.

"Mommy?" James spoke up.

"Yes, dear," Anna replied.

"Why when the king invited all the people from the street to be a part of the wedding, did he toss out the guy who was not dressed like everyone else?"

"Well, James, Jesus is actually referring to the kingdom of heaven. To this kingdom, He calls everyone. But not everyone will be chosen. This man at the wedding banquet knew what was expected of him. And since he did not do as what was expected, the king got rid of him," Anna answered. "Do you understand?" James shook his head indicating he still did not get the parable.

"You see…" Anna continued, "it is not enough to hear the call of Jesus. We must do what is expected of us if we are to enter into the kingdom of heaven."

With a somber look, James slowly nodded and finally understood. "Okay, time for bed you two."

Eric and James slowly rose and headed off to their room. "Don't forget to say your prayers."

"Okay, Mom," they returned.

That night, after prayers, James turned to his brother. "How will I know what is expected of me?"

Eric answered, "You'll know. Jesus will let you know."

The following day was a very wet and rainy one. It was a constant rain that seemed like it would never let up. As the rain fell, James was staring out the window. There was not much else to do. Eric came up from behind.

"Wanna learn poker?" he asked.

"That game you and Daddy play?" James inquired.

"Yes."

"I can try. It looks tough though."

"Not really," Eric reassured him. "Come on, I'll show you."

They sat at the table and Eric pulled out some chips. "The white ones are worth one dollar, the red ones are worth five dollars and the blue ones are ten dollars," Eric explained.

"Do I get the money when I'm done?" James asked jovially.

"I wish," Eric retorted. "Now, you will be dealt five cards. Then you will have a choice to get rid of up to three cards. After that, you bet on your hand. If your bet is called, you both turn over your cards and the best hand will win."

"How will I know what to get rid of?"

"That is based on what hand you are going for."

"Hand?"

"Yes, there are nine winning hands in poker. Some say that there is ten, but I'll explain that later."

As Eric went through each hand, he pulled out an example from the deck. "Your first hand is called a 'high card'. If you can make no other hand, then you go by the highest card in your hand."

On the table he laid out an example with a seven, a three, a nine, a five and an ace of all different suits.

"See it?"

James nodded. Eric took away one card and replaced it with a new card that demonstrated the next hand on the list. This went on all the way up to the royal flush. When he got there, Eric paused for a moment.

"The reason that they say there are ten hands is that they count the royal flush as a hand all of its own. Really it is just the highest straight flush you can get. Course, if you get this hand, you are guaranteed to win." James smiled before Eric continued. "No hand can beat this. Now, before any cards are dealt everyone must put in an ante, which is just a dollar."

Eric tossed in a white chip and James followed. After a quick shuffle, Eric dealt out the cards. They each gathered up the small pile of cards in front of them. After a few moments of organizing and moving them around, Eric looked up. "How many would you like?" he asked.

"How many would I like?"

"Yes, you can toss up to three cards face down and get up to three cards back."

"Oh..." James stated, "I don't want any then."

"Are you sure?" Eric questioned.

"Yup," James replied with a smile.

"Okay..." After a pause, Eric spoke up again. "I'll take two." After he drew his two cards and rearranged his hand, he looked up at his brother.

"Now you can bet any amount you want."

James tossed in a blue chip.

Eric called the bet. "I have two pair," he said as he turned over his cards.

"I believe I've got you," James replied as he turned over his cards to reveal a royal flush. Which happened to be the same one that Eric had demonstrated moments earlier.

"Beginner's luck, Jimmy," Eric commented. As the day rained on, Eric and James sat at the table playing cards. At one point, John sat in with them and played a few hands. And although James picked up the mechanics of poker fairly quickly, the subtleties of the art of bluffing and playing your opponent rather than playing your cards eluded him.

The following day, the sun was shining through a few sporadic puffy white clouds. The boys finished their chores as quickly as they could. And once they were completed, Eric and James grabbed their cane poles and ran out the door. Anna called after them. "Eric… wait for your brother!"

James was running behind. "Hey, wait up!" James caught up to his brother and they were soon walking together.

"One of these days I hope I'm as good as you at shootin'," James said.

"Well, it just takes practice, Jimmy. As Daddy said, don't rush it. It'll come."

They continued through a meadow that was covered in wildflowers of all varied species and colors. And even though they were of different shapes and sizes, they all moved in perfect symmetry with the wind. A few small white moths floated effortlessly through the air. A carpenter bee flew from one flower to another looking for some sweet nectar. Up in the sky, a passing red tail hawk glided on a thermal current without a care in the world. And above the carefree hawk, a few white puffy clouds continued to dot the otherwise bright blue canopy. On the other side of the meadow was a forest. Eric and James slipped through the trees and followed a small path. This path, strewn with roots and rocks, led down to a river. The level of the river's height was raised from the prolonged rainstorm the day before. But even with that change, Eric and James, who had been there several times before, still knew the best spots to fish.

"First one to catch a fish, wins!" James challenged his brother. Eric agreed and they went to it. As the hour pressed on, they were both still in pursuit of that elusive first fish. Then, in a fleeting moment, the silence was broken by the well—known excitement in a voice that echoed off the plethora of trees.

"I GOT ONE!" James called out as his cane pole arced towards the water. "I GOT ONE!"

Eric pulled his line out of the water and headed over to get a glimpse of the first catch of the afternoon. And it was a beautiful catch. A speckled brown trout that was almost ten inches in length from head to tail.

"Nice one Jimmy. Let's string 'im up."

Together they rigged up a string to hold the defenseless fish. Once it was secured, they returned to their poles and continued fishing. It was not long before James' excited voice rang out again. "I got another one!" After a moment the excitement went away. "Oh man, never mind. I'm snagged." James added. Eric looked over in the direction of his brother's voice.

"Can you get it out?"

"Yeah, I think so," James replied.

"I'd better go check it out just in case," Eric said under his breath. With that thought, he placed his cane pole on the ground and headed over towards his brother. While he was en route, Eric heard his brother's scream followed by the sound of a large object landing in the river. James, while trying to free his cane pole, lost his balance and fell into the river. For whatever reason, he still held on to it and the way he landed in the water freed up his line. However, he was now being swept away by the river's current. Eric ran along the bank of the river as fast as he could. Through his perseverance, he managed to get ahead of his brother who was trying to call out to him for help. Eric waded out into the river with one hand holding on to a tree branch that hung out over the water. With his other hand, Eric was able to reach out and grab his younger brother. As James held on, Eric helped him to the river's edge and onto the bank. After they emerged from the river, they both collapsed on the dry ground under their knees.

"Thanks for saving my life," James said gratefully.

"Don't mention it," Eric gave back. "Besides, you would have done the same for me."

In the back of his mind, James knew his brother was absolutely right. After a few moments of lying there on the ground, Eric looked over. A surprised look came over his face as he looked over at the cane pole in his brother's hand.

"Well, how about that," Eric stated.

"How about what?"

Then James looked down at his pole. At the end of his line was another fish frantically flopping in the dirt.

"You *do* have another one."

The two children then erupted into a burst of uncontrollable laughter. When the moment had passed, they got to their feet and went back to the spot where they'd started out that afternoon. That night, as the family enjoyed the fish the boys had caught, Eric regaled them with the story of James' miraculous catch.

A few days later the boys were outside in the woods near their house. On this day the two adventurous youths were building a trap to ensnare a rabbit or a squirrel or some other small creature.

"Do you think it will work?" James asked hopefully.

"Oh yeah," Eric said confidently, "but we need to find a good spot."

James looked around. "How do you know a good spot?" he asked. Eric looked around.

"Come with me and I will show you."

They walked through the woods as Eric's eyes surveyed the wooded area.

"What are you looking for?" James questioned inquisitively.

"To catch a rabbit, you need to find their home and entice the rabbit to come out of his hole."

After a few moments more, Eric stopped. He placed his hand on his brother's chest signaling him to stop moving. "Shh…" he whispered, "there's the hole."

They quietly crept over to the hole and meticulously set the trap near it. The two siblings took a step back and looked around for a place to hide. There was a thick tree that seemed more than adequate for them to hide. They made their way over and scurried behind it, out of sight of the trap. And there they sat. Occasionally they would peer around the massive trunk to see if their trap were sprung. Each time they noticed no change at all. James was getting restless and could not just sit still any more. So, he stood up and dusted off his backside.

"Where are you going?" Eric inquired.

"I'm getting bored. I'm gonna go climb that tree over there." James answered. The tree was not too far off and so Eric saw no problem with it.

"Just be careful, Jimmy. And quiet." Eric requested. "I wanna catch a rabbit today."

James agreed with his brother and moseyed off to climb his tree. Eric rested his back against the rough bark of the ancient resident of the forest and kept watch on the trap and his brother. James was enjoying his climb as he slowly ascended the massive tree. He felt the joy and excitement we all feel inside as we climb higher and higher. And the sturdy pillar of wood and leaves did not seem to mind the young and enthusiastic boy whose hands and feet clambered about. But his happiness was cut short. When James was about twenty feet up in the tree, a branch under his foot snapped. It happened so quickly that he could not react and support himself. As he began to plummet to the forest floor, James let out the most harrowing and bloodcurdling scream that echoed harshly through the trees. Eric sprang to his feet. Panic, fear and adrenaline surged through his body as he frantically raced to the tree his brother was once a part of. James landed with a thud on the soft, mossy floor below. Luckily, there were no rocks or protruding roots where his body came to rest. When he reached his brother, Eric looked on in fear. But a few moments later, James opened his eyes and started talking.

"Did we catch a rabbit?"

Eric looked on.

"No," he replied as the adrenaline started to wear off. "Come on... let's get you home."

Eric bent down and scooped up his brother. As he started the walk home with his brother in his arms, James looked at him.

"You're always there for me when I need you."

To this, Eric responded by telling him, "That's what brothers are for."

Eric carried his brother most of the way, taking breaks every so often to catch his breath and take a short rest. When they were close to their house, James asked to be put down.

"Are you sure?" Eric asked.

"Yeah... I'm fine," James reassured him, "Besides, I don't want Mom to worry."

Eric agreed and carefully placed his brother on the ground. They walked together the rest of the way home. Eric and James agreed not to tell their mother or father about the incident with the tree that afternoon. They felt that there was no reason to bring it up since James was okay.

Time moved on and days went by. It was another beautiful sunny afternoon when James and Eric asked their father if they could shoot again. As John agreed to his boys' request, he noticed a disapproving look from his wife.

"You two go on outside and wait for me. I'll be by directly." When the two boys exited the house and John heard the front door close, he turned back to his wife. "What is it, honey?"

"I just don't like the idea of them and guns, John," Anna replied.

"Why not?"

"I'm afraid they may go off and follow your old path," Anna answered with a degree of worry. "And they may not be as fortunate as you were."

"Anna, I'm not just teaching them to shoot. I'm teaching them to defend themselves. This world is getting worse every day. And I do not want our boys to be unprepared for its decay. I did not have such a teacher when I was growing up. Plus, thanks to you they also know of Jesus and the path He walked. I believe that with my teachings and those you impart from Jesus, that they will never end up like I was before I met you."

"I'm just scared for my babies, John."

"I know," John said comfortingly. "Which is why I want them to be able to protect themselves."

Although Anna was disheartened, she knew he was right. John took up his pistols and headed outside to where his two boys were anxiously waiting.

That night they enjoyed supper together as usual. There was laughter and much talking. And such a fun time it was. But none of them knew that this would be the last meal that they would ever share together. If so, maybe they would have said more meaningful things. Or in their prayer to give thanks for the meal, they might have asked that it never would end. But the meal did end, and life went on as it usually did. After the meal, Eric and James and Anna were engrossed in the New Testament. They were reading about the parable of the talents. Once again, James was confused and did not understand the meaning behind it.

"Why did the master punish the servant who buried his master's talent to keep it safe until the master came home?"

Anna looked at her son. She was very pleased that he was asking such questions to glean more knowledge. "You see, God has given each one of us talents. What matters is what we do with these talents. In this case, the servant who had buried his talent is someone who, in a sense, wasted the talent that God had given him. The master felt betrayed by the servant for wasting his talent. James, God gave us the gift of eternal life. A gift He gave to all of us. But it is not enough to just receive this gift. It is what we do with the knowledge of that gift. If we accept the gift and do nothing, then we are not worthy of that gift. But if we receive that same gift with honor and share the knowledge of that gift through God's teachings, we become worthy and will be graciously accepted into the kingdom of heaven," Anna explained.

James gave an understanding smile. They continued to read a few more passages before it was time for bed once again. After bedtime prayers, the two boys laid there until they finally drifted off to sleep. John and Anna also drifted off into a peaceful slumber.

The night was dark and cloudy. Occasionally a gap in the clouds would allow the light from the moon to shine through and fall on the otherwise darkened silhouette of the house and the surrounding land.

In the darkness, a small group of men moved about the front of the house. One of the men slowly made his way up to the front door. While he was en route, John had woken up. Something inside was telling him that something was wrong. As he carefully climbed out of bed, Anna, who was fast asleep, rolled over onto her side. John quietly grabbed his holster and fastened it around his waist. Then, as soft as a mouse's footsteps, he traversed the room to the door. Just as the man was about to knock on it, John opened the door slowly.

"Can I help you?" John asked.

"Are you John Harper?" the stranger inquired.

"Yes," John answered. "Can I help you?"

"This is for ratting out my brother!" As the stranger spoke, he raised a rifle and fired at close range. As the stranger lifted the rifle, John drew his pistol. But it was not until he hit the ground that John fired a shot that struck the stranger between his eyes. Eric and James leapt from their beds and ran to the bedroom door. Immediately Eric ran to his fallen father. John, knowing he was all but dead, whispered to his son.

"Pro- tect... them... a... ven... avenge... m... me..."

As he spoke, John handed the pistol in his grip to his son. As John's last breath filled his lungs and then slowly escaped, James ran to his side.

"DADDY!"

Eric looked at his brother. Knowing that now was not the time to grieve, he took the pistol that was in his hand and passed it over to James.

"Go," Eric said sternly. "Take this and go and protect Mom."

James, who was still stunned spoke up, "But..."

"No buts Jimmy. Go. Now. Before it's too late."

Reluctant to leave his father's side and shattered at his death, James got up. He knew his brother was right.

"What are you gonna do?"

"Kill 'em all, Jimmy. Kill 'em all."

James went to his mother's side. Anna was in stark disbelief at all that had transpired. Perhaps under different circumstances, she would be exceptionally proud of the bravery, composure and the actions of her boys and the way that they handled this crisis. But that was not the case.

"Mommy, come," James said. "We gotta hide."

Anna, still in shock, was led back into the darkness of her bedroom. This was the day that she never wanted or ever wanted her boys to see or be a part of. But you do not always get what you pray for. Back near the front, Eric had taken up his father's other pistol. He then pinned his back next to the front door. Carefully, he peered out through the now-infamous opening and saw the stranger sprawled out on the front porch... dead. If there were words to describe what was coursing through his heart and his mind and his body, they would be placed here. But all the rage in the world, all that and more would not do justice to the anger within him. Eric managed to slither outside and move next to the dead stranger. He unfastened and removed that varmint's holster and strapped it on himself. Then his hand stretched out and his fingers slowly surrounded the instrument of his father's death — the rifle that took his father's life — and made his way to the side of the house. With his back firmly against the wall, he looked up to the darkened sky.

"Lord. Let my shot be true that I might strike down these vipers."

And as if the Lord had heard his prayer, and answered it, there was a break in the clouds. This break also brought the moon's light to the house and the land before it. With this light, Eric could see three men slowly walking to the house.

With his fear and nerve in check, Eric lifted the rifle and took his aim. And the moment that he had prayed for was not on him. As his finger squeezed the cold metal of the trigger, a chain reaction was started. The hammer slid back slowly. And when it reached the apex of its path, it raced forward with all its might. The hammer came to rest as it struck its target. At this point, the explosion of the black powder within the shell ignited inside and propelled the bullet down the length of the barrel and ejected it with a forceful plume of smoke from the other side. The bullet hurtled through the air as fast as bullets do. Within seconds of when this process was started, the bullet lodged itself within the chest of the man in the middle. As he collapsed, the other two men ran back for cover. Once there, they and the other two guys with them opened fire with a fury of bullets. These bullets relentlessly attacked the house before them. Glass shattered and furniture was destroyed. When they stopped to reload their weapons, Eric knew this was his chance. He fired the rifle while he was moving away from the house. It was his attempt at luring his enemies from the house. As the two men saw his silhouette in the moonlight, one turned to the other.

"Get him. And see that he joins his father."

"No problem," the other man replied as he headed off in pursuit. By this time Eric had made it to the tree line and disappeared within. He saw the man who was sent off after him and fired once again. This shot unfortunately missed its target. The man attempted to return fire while moving which caused his shot to also miss. Eric continued to run through the trees. Although he had played amongst these trees all of his life, none of them seemed the least bit familiar to him tonight. He paused to listen for his stalker and when he heard the snap of a dry branch in the distant darkness, he turned and fired. The man quickly slid behind a tree.

"Come out kid. I'll make it easy on you."

Eric's only answer was another blast from the barrel. He then started running again. The light of the moon had broken through the clouds again. And its light, though scattered through the branches of the trees above him had shed light on the forest floor. Not only did its light shine on the ground, but the moon also illuminated the silhouette of a boy running through the woods. The man saw him and believed that now was his opportunity to rid himself of this nuisance. But what happened next must have been divinely orchestrated from the universe because it all happened in absolute perfect timing. Just as the man pulled the trigger to expel one more round from his rifle, Eric's foot hit a root. This caused him to fall into a small ravine that was before him. The way Eric's body flailed as he fell convinced the other man that his shot was the cause and that his chase was over.

Meanwhile, back at the house, another man made his way to the front door. He was not sure if anyone else was still alive inside, so he proceeded with a cautious step. He moved past the two dead men that were lying in front of the house. Shattered glass crumbled with an eerie sound as he walked through the seemingly vacant abode. He walked past the table where they ate their last meal. Around the corner, he peered into the room where Eric and James had rested their heads so peacefully every night until tonight. Seeing nothing, he continued to wander through the house, passing through the living room. As he walked, his foot pushed against a book that was on the floor. Carelessly moving it aside, he continued on to the other side of the shattered place. As he approached Anna and John's bedroom, James and his mother tried to remain silent. Soon, a tall, dark figure appeared in the doorway. Without a second thought, James fired a shot. The bullet had pierced the left shoulder of the tall silhouette. The man screamed in pain. With vengeful fervor, he twisted his arm around the frame of the door and unloaded every round within his pistol. There was no aiming, just random shooting. And although his shooting had no real direction, two of the bullets struck James' mother. Anna's body flew backwards on her son, causing him to fall back too. On his way back, he hit his head. This, though painful and rendering him unconscious, is what saved his life. His father's pistol had slipped from his hand and slid under the bed. The lone assailant waiting outside the room heard the thud of their bodies as they landed on the floor. He cautiously peered around the door jamb. The obscured moonlight that seeped in through the windows revealed Anna's lifeless body. Satisfied that she was reunited with her husband as well, he turned to leave. As he made his way out the door and passed the body of his comrade, his partner who had chased down Eric made his way across the lawn. The others came up from their spot as well.

"Did you get him Dave?" the man on the porch called out.

"Oh, he's worm food now," Dave happily replied. "We done here?"

"Yup," responded the leader as he joined his men. "Let's get outta here."

With that, the small group of men made off in high spirits for they had accomplished their objective.

What could have been hours was merely half of one. When Eric came to, he slowly lifted his head to look around. After seeing and hearing nothing, he raised himself off the ravine floor. Wiping away leaves and mud, he cleaned himself off. Bending over, Eric took up the rifle. After being certain that he still had his father's pistol, he climbed out of the ravine. The clouds were all but gone now and the moon illuminated his way home.

Uncertain of what he would find there, Eric held his father's pistol tightly and was intently ready to fire. When he made it to the house he had built so many fond memories in, everything was shattered. There was no joy, no happiness left in his world. As he passed his father's body, even though he already knew it to be dead, extreme sadness overtook him. Slowly, Eric made his way to where his parents used to sleep. And even though he tried to prepare himself for what he knew would lie in store, no amount of preparation could ever set him up for the sight of the two lifeless bodies on the floor. Anna, his mother, the one who had brought him into this world, who nurtured, cared for and loved him with every breath she took would take no more. And there, beneath her slumped body was the lifeless corpse of his younger, brother James, whom he had sworn to protect and loved most of all. The torment was too much as tears rolled down his cheeks. The overwhelming sadness was soon replaced with an unwavering and purely determined vengeance for those responsible. He headed back to the front door. After a pause to bid farewell to his father, he stood up once more. He walked over to the evil bastard who'd taken his father's life. With fury in his heart, Eric raised the rifle and took aim. And even though this man was already dead, Eric felt the compelling need to fire one last shot into the face of this monster. As he pulled the trigger, Eric stated with force, "Rot in hell you son of a bitch!" As the shot echoed across the trees, Eric's destiny was now set in stone. He would not rest until all those who had a hand in this night's tragedy were punished and cut down from the earth. With his mind thus set, he headed off into the night. In the distance, a lone wolf's solemn howl reverberated through the darkness.

The following early morning light brought nature to life. And all around the land, it was peaceful and serene. Almost as if nature itself had turned a blind eye to the atrocity which befell the land the night before. Birds were chirping away, happily looking for food or something to add to their nest. A few bees were pleasantly buzzing about from one flower to the next. A lone rabbit was enjoying the leaves of a small clover patch. And the sun, whose light was on all of nature's beauty, also made its way into the window of the bedroom where James and his mother lay together. A cardinal landed on the windowsill and its song had woken James from his sleep. The first thought in his mind was that the horrors of the night before were nothing but a horrible nightmare. But as his eyes opened and he saw the gleam of his father's pistol there under the bed, he knew it was real. He looked down to see his mother's head resting so peacefully on his chest. And though he knew that she was no longer with him in this world, he tried to wake her up. However, nobody but Jesus could wake the dead. With this disheartening thought in mind, James carefully lifted her head and slowly moved from under her. Then, even more carefully, he laid her head back down on the floor. He reached under the bed and took up his father's pistol. Walking out into the living room, James noticed the book that had been carelessly kicked aside by his assailant last night. The binding was scarred and some of the pages were folded. He picked it up and closed it carefully. In doing so he noticed that there was a bullet hole through the cover. However, through all its damages, the title of the book could still be seen: The Holy Bible. As he came into the kitchen where the front door was, he saw the body of his father. James lay the Bible and his father's pistol on the kitchen table and then knelt down before his father's corpse. With a solemn and sad disposition, he slowly removed his father's holster. Placing it on the table near the Bile and pistol, James took his first steps outside. There he saw two bodies more. The one laid out on the porch and the other one sprawled out on the grass. In a desperate attempt and with feeble hopes of success James called out, "ERIC!" He looked around and hollered once more for his brother. But the only response he got was a startled blue jay and the echo of his own sullen voice. And it finally sank in that he was now completely alone. He looked around through heavy tears as all that was taken from him. He sat there for what could have been an eternity for him though it was only a mere fraction of that time. James knew what he must do next though the task was, to him, more difficult than all the struggles the apostles shared in the Bible.

He went back into the house and returned to the front porch with a shovel. With it, he began to dig. Slowly at first, but then his pace quickened. He stopped a few times to take breaks for some water before returning to his task. On finishing the second hole in the ground, he had to stop. His hands were sore and calloused. His determination was strong, as was his will, but his young body could not keep up. Jamming the shovel into a mound of dirt, James ventured into the house. He was there just long enough to eat some bread. He then returned to the porch with his food. And although it was no breakfast of champions, the bread satisfied his hunger and James was soon back with the shovel. As he completed the third hole, he once again jammed the shovel into a mound of dirt. Furthering his strength, James went first to his father. And though he struggled to drag his father's body, James managed to bring him to the first hole he had dug. Saddened, he rolled his father's lifeless body into the shallow grave. He had to pause for his strength to return before he could even attempt to bring his mother out. When he finally gained strength and composure, he rose and returned to the house. To see his mother there was more torture than he could bear. Uncontrollable tears poured down his cheeks like a waterfall over a cliff. And with every tug of his mother's body, the emotions surged forward. It seemed it took forever just to get her body out of the bedroom. Part of James' soul pleaded with him to stop and just leave. But for whatever reasons remained, he knew he had to finish what he had started. And with that determination, James struggled on. Finally, he reached the front door and paused again for a breath. For now, the tears had seemed to subside and soon he had his poor mother's body on the grass. Pulling and tugging, he reached the second hole and rolled his mother into that shallow grave. The third shallow grave would remain empty as he did not have the body to fill it. James then grabbed the shovel and began to cover his father's body. When the body was covered and the mound was complete, he began to shovel dirt on the remains of his mother. For anyone to bury their parents after such a tragedy would be very difficult. But for a young boy of only seven, it was worse than purgatory itself. Slowly but surely, he covered his mother's corpse. The third hole, though empty, still brought tears to him, not only because he had lost his brother, but also the fact that he didn't have a body to lay within the grave. Finally, the third grave was filled in. There were only two things left to do now. He placed the shovel against the house and made his way to the trees. Once there, he took up six branches and brought them back to the house. He went inside and soon emerged with some string and a knife. He laid out the first two branches and used some of the string to lash them together. When this was finished, he repeated his actions with the remaining branches. He then took the three crosses that he had fashioned and placed each one at the top of each new grave. When this was finished, James went into the house one last time.

He donned his father's holster and placed the only remaining pistol within it. He took up his mother's Bible and then returned to their graves. He stood before them and spoke through falling tears.

"I... know I m-must say goodbye. But I do not know how to do it. I know that... when I leave... this... this place, that I will take you with me. A-and I pray that the Lord keep... you and c-care for you. And I pray... that you will watch over me." He choked up hard before saying one last thing. "Goodbye."

On that note, he turned and walked away. He had no idea where he was going; all he knew was that he would never return to this place he once happily called home. The sun by now was setting low in the sky. A brilliant reddish hue painted the clouds so vividly that even van Gogh would be enamored by its harmonious synchronicity. James continued on his way and soon night had fallen. James kept on walking. He was determined to put as much distance as he could between where he was now and the desolation and destruction he left behind. He came to what could be considered a road and blindly chose a direction. Though his pace was steady, there was a spring in his step. The night grew longer as James trudged on. Even when he was feeling exhausted, he refused to stop. It was almost as if he was hoping that one more step would be his last and that he could see his mother once again. Or play with his brother in the forest. The sky began to lighten when his exhaustion finally overtook him. He collapsed to the ground, still clutching the Bible he brought from home. The only thing he brought with him except for his father's pistol by his side. The sun was starting to peek over the trees. The soft light illuminated a beautiful two-story house. This house was owned by a man named Alex Lorin. He had moved from London's east side to the county just outside of Dry River as a boy with his father after his mother passed away. His father apprenticed as a banker and before his death, took ownership of the bank. On his death, ownership was transferred to Alex who continued to successfully maintain it even in times of civil unrest. Now, he was in his mid-forties; a short and portly bearded man. His wife Sarah was no taller than he was albeit much thinner and of average appearance. She would remain at the house while Alex was at work. As was the standard of the time, she would cook and clean and also take care of their daughter Katherine. Upstairs in her room, Katherine was just getting out of her bed. Her dirty blonde hair was past her shoulders and had slight waves of curls throughout. She was also seven years old. Her room, although small, had a window that overlooked the front of the house. As she stood there taking in the morning sun, she felt its warmth fill her. Off to one side, she could see her father's horse walking through the grass. He would occasionally drop his head to graze some grass before moving on to another part of the fenced-in field. At times her father would put her in the saddle and walk her around the pasture. Some day she hoped to ride that horse on her own. And in time, that day would come. Until then, Katherine was satisfied with being led around by her father.

"Katie…" her mother called from the base of the stairs. "Time for breakfast."

"Okay, Mother," Katherine replied happily. She easily shed her pajamas and took up a white sundress. As it slipped past her head and came to rest on her shoulders, she happened to glance back out her window.

Off in the distance along the side of the road, she noticed an odd lump. She could not tell whether it was an animal or not. But the birds that circled nearby led her to deduce that it was some form of food for them. Through curiosity, she moved closer to the window and strained harder to see. She could barely make out a rectangular object. On an assumption, she hurried to finish getting dressed. She pulled on her shoes and went as fast as she could out of her bedroom and down the stairs. Sarah had heard the commotion of her daughter. However, by the time Sarah had reached the stairs, Katherine was already at the front door.

"Katie dear, you need to eat before you go outside." Her mother called out. But Katherine proceeded to open the front door. It was not that she was intentionally choosing to ignore her mother, but in her hurried state, she did not even hear Sarah's request. She ran down to the road and as she got closer, her suspicion was correct.

"Father! Father! Come here! Quick!" she hollered out. Alex, on hearing the urgency in his daughter's voice, came running from the back of the house. Sarah was still standing there at the front door as her father rounded the corner and headed out the door to where his daughter was standing. As he got closer, he too saw the odd lump in the road. It was a small boy who appeared to be around the same age as his daughter. This forced him to run even faster. When he reached the two of them, he knelt down and did a cursory inspection. On this, it was clear that the boy was still alive. As Alex scooped the boy up from the road he looked to his daughter.

"Go inside and fetch some water and a cloth."

Katherine picked up the rectangular object and hurried inside. Alex carried the small boy across the lawn and into the house. As he passed his wife, Sarah, fearing the worst, spoke up.

"Is he...?" she could not even finish the sentence due to the nature of the thought that preceded it.

"No... he's still alive." Sarah breathed a heavy sigh of relief and went off to get some water. Alex proceeded to lay the boy on their sofa. Sarah ran into her daughter while en route and saw that Katherine had already procured the items she was about to fetch. They returned to the living room.

"Here Daddy."

"Thank you, sweetie."

With a careful hand, he gently washed the dirt from the boy's face and hands. Still, the child did not stir.

Alex removed the holster which held one lone pistol from around the boy's waist. He handed it to his wife.

"Here, Sarah," he said, "put this somewhere safe." Katherine offered up the rectangular object to her mother.

"And this too?" she asked. Alex gently took it from her.

"No." He rested the scarred Bible on the ottoman next to the sofa. "This we will leave with him."

After breakfast, Katherine went to the boy's side. She stood vigil and would periodically wipe down his face. Alex and Sarah were surprised at their daughter's dedication to taking care of the boy. Another hour had passed when his eyes slowly began to open. Through his groggy and blurred vision, the first thing he saw was Katherine's face as she was leaning over him and caressing his face with the cool damp cloth.

He mustered the strength to speak.

"Are… you an… angel?" he uttered. Though only seven, she was flattered by the question.

"No. My name is Katie." With a smile, she asked for his name.

"Ja-James."

Alex came around the corner and saw the boy moving.

"Well look who's awake," he said. "Would you like to eat something?"

"Not… real-really hungry, sir," James replied.

"Nonetheless, I'll have my wife put something on for you just in case you change your mind." James sat up. "What's your name son?"

"His name is James, Daddy," Katherine interjected with a smile.

"Well James, my name is Alex Lorin." He pointed over to his wife. "My wife, Sarah. And it looks as though you already met my daughter Katherine."

"Y-yes sir I have," James responded. It started to become easier to speak as his exhaustion was starting to fade. Sarah knelt down with a bowl of stew and a small piece of bread. She handed it off to James who, even though he claimed not to be hungry, slowly began to eat. With each spoonful, he began to perk up more and soon the bowl was emptied. Sarah took up the bowl and returned it to the kitchen. James' strength had all but fully returned. However, the emotional scars would remain for some time. James looked around for a few moments and then reached down to his side to notice that the holster and pistol were missing. This caused a frantic panic as he looked quickly around his body. "Wh... where is it?" he asked.

"Relax, James. I have it in a safe place. You won't need it for now. But I will return it to you before you leave," Alex said reassuringly.

The knowledge that the pistol was safe was a comfort to him. Sarah came back into the living room.

"Where are your parents, James?" she inquired.

Saddened by the answer that he had to reveal, James struggled to hold back the tears as he responded, "They're dead. Along with my brother Eric."

Sarah's hand slowly rose to her face and her fingers loosely covered her mouth.

"I'm so sorry." Now she was fighting back tears. Seeing the bloodstained clothes and the damage to the Bible on the ottoman, Alex felt compelled to push for more information.

"What happened?" he asked.

"Well, I guess it was two nights ago now. My brother and I heard a loud bang. We heard voices and then my father's pistol. My brother ran to my father as I tried to as well. He gave me one of the pistols and told me to hide with Mom. He then ran out the door and I heard some shots. As I hid with my mother, I heard someone. I fired and I missed. He shot my mother. She fell back on me and that's all I remember. When I woke up, she was dead. So was my father. I buried them and left with that and my father's gun."

By the end of the recounting, both Sarah and Katherine were in tears.

"I walked as far as I could. Then I woke up here."

"And your brother? He never made it back?" Alex inquired.

"No," James answered through tears. "They shot him as he tried to save us."

Sarah was at a complete loss for words. Alex, knowing he did not even need to ask, spoke up, "Well, you are going to live with us now. You can attend school with Katie. I will make the arrangements."

James, who up to this point had lost everything, felt a small degree of comfort from the kindness that they showed him.

"I'll make some clothes for you," Sarah added.

"Thank you, ma'am," James replied. Katherine looked over at him.

"You want to see my Daddy's horse, Jimmy?" she asked pleasantly. Feeling a small amount of his depression lifting, he agreed. Katherine reached out her hand and with him in tow, they headed outside. After they were gone, Sarah looked down at her husband who was just starting to stand up.

"I cannot believe what that poor child has been through!" she sadly exclaimed.

"I know, Sarah. I know." Alex looked out the window. "But you know, I think he'll be okay." Outside, Katherine and James were standing by the fence, watching the horse, a beautiful specimen with a shining brown coat and black mane. It was almost as if the horse knew he had an audience because he began to run through the field and in some ways seem to show off his own personality. He would slow down to a gentle canter and then break into a full sprint only to slow back down again.

"One day I'm going to ride him all by myself," Katherine said with certainty. James looked over.

"I've never ridden a horse before."

"Never?"

"Uh-uh. Never."

"Well, I'm sure Daddy will let you on him if you would like to try."

"I would," James responded. "It looks like it would be a lot of fun."

They remained there, hanging on the fence, talking about all the things that a seven-year-old finds interesting or important.

The following day, Katherine walked with James to the schoolhouse. It was a quaint little one-room affair. The teacher was already informed of James' situation, and she rearranged the seating so that James could sit next to Katherine. They felt that this would help make him feel a little more comfortable. And it did help a little.

During recess, James and Katherine were sitting alone and just talking about nothing of real importance. And as with every school, there is usually a bully. This school was no different. His name was Jared. And as usual, it was customary for the bully to 'announce' himself to the new kid. Because this is the nature of schools, that is what Jared did. Now, Jared was not any bigger than James, but he was definitely not so much a nice individual. He began slinging insults and taunting James and Katherine. She implored him to just move on and leave them alone. This plea made Jared push even harder on the insults. James just sat there with no reaction at all. It would only be a matter of time before

Jared went too far. And it happened. Jared made a crack about James' mother. That was the final word on insults. Katherine jumped to her feet and quickly pushed Jared away. She knew what James had been through and this was one subject that should have been left alone. This shove from Katherine caused Jared to shove back. James immediately sprung up and quicker than a snake could grab a mouse, James' fist landed right in Jared's stomach. As Jared bent over in pain, James grabbed his shirt and tossed him into the nearby tree. By this time the teacher had made her way over, but the damage had already been done. They were each taken inside where the teacher asked for the details. Katherine spoke up about the crack insult that Jared made about James' mother. The teacher, also knowing what had happened to his family and what James had been through, was sympathetic. In knowing that Jared was the class bully, a small part of her was glad to see him get a taste of it. But she could not let on about that. Instead, she played her part and made them each apologize and promise not to cause any other issues. To this end, they did so. But what seemed to be a hapless apology shifted. James and Jared actually became friends. It seems that a beat down is all it takes from time to time. And as time went on, the three of them actually became inseparable. Especially James and Katherine.

When they had finished their schooling, Katherine's father gave James a job at the bank in Dry River. Now Dry River was a quaint small town, aptly named for the dried-up river bed nearby. At the south end of the town, the river had carved through and formed a canyon. This had happened centuries before. Before the town was founded, the river shifted geologically and moved underground. For this, all that was left was the remnants of its ancient past. The town itself was fairly nice. The citizens were all content with the peace and happiness that seemed to hover over the town. The saloon was clean and rarely had trouble. And of course, the law that prohibited individuals from carrying firearms within the town's limits helped to sway issues. It was a widely accepted law amongst the citizens of Dry River. However, there are always exceptions to every rule. And sometimes it was apparent that someone would not wish to abide by the rule. One afternoon, James was working at the bank as he had usually done. Alex was getting ready to lock up. As he made his way to the front door, it slowly opened. A man walked in with a casual demeanor.

"We're getting ready to close up for the day, sir," Alex stated. "Can I assist you?" The man closed the door behind him. After this, he turned back to Alex. With a sly grin, the man pulled out a pistol.

"I'm here for a withdrawal."

Alex froze in fear of the pistol that was pointed in his direction. James, who stood behind the counter, watched to scene unfold. The man reached out and grabbed Alex by the arm and forced him to the counter.

"Put the cash in a sack. Now!" the man ordered.

He stood about two inches taller than Alex and spoke with a rough voice. It was apparent that he was not a local to the town; rather, he was just some drifting vagrant trying to make a quick buck. James cautiously grabbed a satchel and began to fill it up slowly to buy time and create an opportunity. James spoke up.

"There's more cash at the other window. Would you like me to grab that too?"

The man did not take long to allow greed to swallow him whole. "What do you think!" the man snapped. "But no tricks!"

After James had filled the satchel with all the cash from his drawer, he made his way to the other window. This window was located right next to the edge of the counter where you would access the window you covered. James filled the bag with all the cash from that window as well. His next move was a risky one. But he had counted on the man's greed to cloud his judgment. When the satchel was filled, James slowly made his way to the edge of the counter where he could slip around. The man kept a small distance and a hold on Alex and the pistol.

"Toss me the bag!" he snapped.

"Point that gun at me and let him go. Then I will toss this bag."

"You're in no position to make any demands!"

"Look," James retorted, "I don't care about the money. I just want to make sure he is safe. So, point that gun at me and let him go. Then you'll get what you came for." The vagrant thought for a moment and figured he had nothing to lose. It did not matter to him who he shot if he had to. With that thought, he trained the gun on James and forcefully pushed Alex to the side. Alex lost his balance and fell to the floor.

"There!" the man screamed, "now give me the money!"

James obliged and tossed the bag rather high in the air. This was his opportunity. The vagabond let his focus shift and his eyes followed the satchel full of cash. With that distraction, he did not see what transpired next. James pulled his pistol and with a single shot, he hit the vagrant's hand that was holding the gun. The shot caused the man to drop his weapon and cradle his newly injured hand. James immediately charged at the man. Digging his shoulder into the would-be robber's solar plexus, he lifted the man off the ground. With the man slumped over James' shoulder, the two men crashed through the door and out into the street. They fell to the ground. The man struggled and tried to get free, but James managed to keep him subdued until the sheriff arrived with his own pistol drawn. The vagrant knew now that there was zero chance of escape and gave up. As the sheriff's deputy cuffed the assailant, James dusted himself off.

"Good job, James," the sheriff commented.

"All in a day's work," James nonchalantly retorted.

"Have you ever thought about being a deputy, James?" The sheriff asked. "I could use someone like you."

James looked over at Alex, who at this time had made his way out of the bank after securing the satchel and then back at the sheriff.

"I work here at the bank. Besides, I would have to talk it over with my fiancée and Alex here."

"Well, the offer is an open invitation. If you ever decide you want it, the job is yours."

The street emptied as the excitement was over and James and Alex made their way back into the bank.

"Sorry about the door, sir," James remarked.

"Don't worry about it, son. The door can be fixed." Alex assured him. "I'm just glad that you're okay. That wasn't a very smart thing to do you know."

"Men like that are always more focused on their greed than on their surroundings."

"What if you were wrong?"

"Well, there was a good chance that he would have shot us both anyhow. And given the two choices, I would rather go down fighting."

"Good point."

With the bank re-secured they made their way home.

"So, are you thinking about the sheriff's offer?"

"Well, it is more money," James said, "but it all depends on Katie."

That night, over dinner, the story was told. Katherine, although proud of her fiancé, was a little concerned. After dinner, the two of them were standing out on the front porch enjoying the calm and warm spring night. Crickets were singing their praises as crickets do. And fireflies seemed to dance to the cricket concerto as they floated carelessly with no apparent sense of direction.

"The sheriff offered me a good opportunity today, to become a deputy."

"What did you say?"

"I told him that I had to talk to you first. I would never take on a job like that without your approval." This was one of the many reasons that Katherine was in love with him. James did not make decisions without considering her opinion and feelings. A rare commodity even in today's society it would seem.

"Well, what do you think you should do?"

"Well…" James replied, "the money is better, but it does come with more of a risk. But I will be honest. It is something that I feel I would be more suited for."

"Are you unhappy with your job at the bank?"

"I am grateful for your father giving me the job. And it does suit us well. And it is just the two of us, so we really don't need the extra money."

"Well actually…" Katherine interjected, "it's not going to be just the two of us."

"It isn't?" James asked curiously. Somewhere in the back of his mind, he knew what she meant. But when he heard Katherine say those two glorious words, 'I'm pregnant', a rush of pure joy and excitement and nervousness swarmed his mind. There were a million things that he wanted to say, but none of them came out. He took Katherine into his arms and held her close. At this point, James did not have to speak. Every word that would have escaped his lips was written in his eyes. And Katherine's heart could read every single one of them.

"So, if you want to take the sheriff's offer, I will be right here by your side."

The next afternoon, James walked out of the sheriff's office with his holster on his side filled with his father's pistol. The small circular badge on his lapel glistened in the sunlight. There was a sense of accomplishment and the overwhelming belief that this was what he was meant to do. This was the path that God had laid out before him. Doing this job is what was expected of him. A week following the acquisition of his new job, Alex and Sarah's backyard was filled with people. Every man was handsomely dressed. Every woman donned a beautiful dress. And not one was without cheer in their heart. With the rows of chairs that covered the yard and the wooden arch at the front of it all, there was no doubt as to what would soon transpire. It was the day that James and Katherine would be united in holy matrimony. Everyone found their seats and James stood at the altar with Jared by his side. Although James knew that Katherine would say yes, he still succumbed to the nervousness that consumed him. And when the woman who would soon acquire his last name appeared, James swore that he had never seen her look more beautiful than right now. At that moment, everyone else disappeared. In his eyes, it was only him and Katherine. And nothing could force him to take his eyes off of her. When the declaration was made, the crowd began to cheer. During the reception that followed, people came up to the two of them and offered their congratulations to the newly wedded couple. That evening, when all of the guests had made their way home, James started to clean up. However, Alex and Sarah would not have it. They made sure that he did not lift a finger for any part of the clean-up. The following day, Alex brought James and Katherine to Dry River. They stopped at the edge of town when Alex spoke up.

"Sarah and I discussed this a few weeks ago and now the time has come."

"Time has come for what Daddy?" Katherine asked.

Alex reached into his pocket and pulled out a set of keys as he spoke.

"Time for you two to have a place of your own." Alex was of course referring to the house at the edge of town. The owner had passed on with no family, so the house went back to the bank. As the owner of the bank, Alex in turn became the owner of that house. Although it was not free and clear, he had the right to do with it as he saw fit.

"You mean…?" Katherine tried to ask excitedly.

"Yes," he responded with a smile, "Sarah and I wanted to give you two something for a wedding gift. Now, you will still have to put some money out for it, but it's yours."

"I don't know how to thank you, sir."

"Please, call me dad. Or Alex. Sir makes me feel old," Alex responded jovially. "And you do not have to thank me, Jimmy. You have made my daughter happy and have blessed us with a grandchild. I couldn't ask for anything more."

James gave Alex a grateful handshake followed by a very warm-hearted hug. When they released from their grip, Katherine frantically threw her arms around her father.

"Thank you so much, Daddy!"

"You're welcome, little one," Alex said. "Just don't forget to come and visit us from time to time. Okay?"

"We will."

James and Katherine walked up to the porch. James unlocked the door. After placing the keys in his pocket, he scooped up his wife and carried her across the threshold. There was a smile on her face that could say far more than old man Webster's book had room for. About a month later, the first deputy came down with a horrible sickness. Unfortunately, there was nothing that could be done to save him from the looming death that followed tuberculosis. The town mourned the loss of the beloved deputy. It was indeed a shame for someone to die so young. But James maintained the position of deputy on his own. And it was not over in the way of tragedies. The sheriff passed away a few months later from a heart attack. James took up the job of sheriff and with that move, there was no deputy. For this, James turned to his best friend Jared. The position was willingly accepted and the two of them made certain that the level of protection that the citizens of Dry River were used to did not waiver. At this time, Katherine's belly had reached its max and before they knew it, a little girl was added to the family. In all, it was twenty—five years since James had lost his family. His daughter, whom they named Sarah after Katherine's mother, was barely a year old now. It was the Fourth of July and the town had its picnic celebration. Some folks were dancing to the music while others were just strolling around. Everyone was happier with the law banning guns within the town limits. And there were only a few times that James had to enforce it. Most times, his trouble revolved around someone getting drunk and out of line. And although he was ready for it tonight, no citizen lost control. After the sun went down, everyone gathered near the north side of town to watch the impressive display of fireworks. James was standing behind the crowd. Katherine had brought Sarah down and as she was Daddy's little girl, when she saw him, she wanted nothing else but him. So, James stood there holding his little princess in one arm and his beautiful wife in his other arm. The fireworks were a spectacular sight and lasted for a decent time. As the crowd cheered to the finale, James kissed his wife.

"Take her to bed," he said as he handed the virtually motionless little bundle to her mother. "I'll be home shortly."

James and Katherine shared one last kiss and then she was off on her way. The rest of the town folks also dispersed saying their farewells and goodnights to their friends and neighbors. The usual men went back to the saloon for whiskey, beer and poker. James wandered the streets just to make sure that all was well. And it was. Overall, it was a quiet and peaceful night.

However, that silence was broken by panicked and frantic screaming from the end of the street. James ran as fast as he could to the origin of the screams to determine the cause and nature of the distress. When he arrived at the end of the street, he could see what caused the commotion. The house at the end of town was ablaze. James turned to Jared.

"Get the men and the water wagon. Meet me up there. Now go!"

"Yes sir!" Jared responded as he turned and ran off. James ran off in the direction of the burning abode. He ran faster than ever before. When he approached the house, the wife and son of five years old were outside working to expel the smoke from their systems.

"Is your husband still inside?" James asked with firmness.

"Yes," the woman gasped. "He tried to help us escape when the floor gave out and he fell through. Can you save him?"

James did not waste time with an answer. He knew that time was of the essence, and he rushed past her and through the front door. What lay before him was a fiery inferno. Flames were dancing all around him. The railing leading up the stairs was glowing as flames raced along it. The door frames were engulfed in yellow and orange wisps that were carelessly feeding on it and rolling across the ceiling were thin waves of flames that looked like a wave rolling on the shore.

"HELLO!" James called out. But there was no answer other than from the fire. And that answer, given through the crackling sounds of burning wood, was that tonight the beast would claim this house. Tonight, the victor wears orange and yellow. James pressed on through the hazardous conditions. He continued to call out but still received no human answer. But his perseverance paid off. He came to where the ceiling gave way. There was a clear view of the second floor. The fire had found its way there as well. As James peered through the disaster, he saw, amidst the debris, the figure of a man. Keeping his composure, he made his way over. Without considering the risk to his own life, James lifted timbers and pulled the man free. As he freed the man from certain death, more of the ceiling started to give way. This time it now blocked their path to the front door. James looked around for another method of egress. He could not get to the window however he noticed off to one side a part of the outside wall that was ablaze. His last-ditch effort proved that his suspicions were correct. The fire had weakened the wall enough that James was able to use his body to break through and reach the outside. When this was accomplished, James ran back through the new door that he had just created and grabbed the man. Lifting him up, James carried him to safety. The town's doctor rushed over to them.

"I'm fine... I'm fine!" James exclaimed through catching up on the fresh air that his lungs desperately wanted, "but he needs help." After a few more coughs and much-appreciated breaths of fresh air, he looked up to the stars. Quietly, almost inaudibly, he uttered 'thank you'.

The man made a full recovery from the inhalation of smoke. The rest of the town helped them to rebuild the house and their life. The fire had started from a few tiny embers that had *leaped* from the fireplace. From there, they had all that they needed to come to life.

A few nights later, James awoke suddenly. He sat up in bed and placed his feet on the floor. It was chilly tonight. In all honesty, it seemed too chilly for this time of year. James rubbed his eyes and then smoothed his hair down. Something did not feel right to him. Something was out of place. But whatever that something was, he could not place his finger on it. He rose from his bed, leaving his wife to sleep. As he walked to the bedroom door, he felt as if he was not home any more, but that he was somewhere that he knew. When he left the bedroom, the memory became a reality. He was back in the living room where he grew up. Without knowing why and with no provocation or reason, he walked to the front door. Without hesitation, his hand reached forward and soon his fingers were on the knob that opened the door. As his hand grabbed it completely, he did what we all would do: he opened the door. As it opened, he saw a dark silhouette of a man holding a rifle. In a horrible and angry voice, he shouted, "IT WAS YOU!". The end of the sentence was followed by the exclamation of the rifle as it fired. As the loud bang resounded, James sat upright in bed. He was home now. In his room, with his wife. Outside though warm, raged a violent yet beautiful thunderstorm. His movements between sitting up in bed and subsequentially climbing out of it woke Katherine from her sleep. As James made his way out of the bedroom, Katherine rose and followed him. James somberly made his way to the front door and headed outside. When Katherine had reached the front door, she saw her husband standing on the edge of the porch looking out into the storm. His hands rested on the porch rail as rain danced on its roof and throughout the dirt-covered street. Katherine knew what had transpired. This was not the first time a nightmare had woken him. In fact, he had many since he was a young boy. Though as he got older, they were not as frequent. She came up behind him and rested her hand on his shoulder. She leaned her head against his arm. Even though she already knew the answer, she asked anyhow.

"Another nightmare?"

"Yeah…" James answered in a voice laced with pain and depression. Trying to console her husband she spoke softly.

"It was just a dream, honey."

"But that just it…" James replied. He quickly raised his hand and slammed it down on the porch rail as he continued speaking. "It wasn't just a dream. It really happened. God, I *wish* it was a dream. And the more I think about it, the more I wonder if it was my fault that my mother died."

"No honey. It was not your fault." Katherine interjected. She knew of his pain and wanted to do all that she could to alleviate it.

"How do you know?" James fired back. "Had I not fired that shot, maybe he would have left thinking the house was empty. It was my shot that told him we were there. Had I not done it she could still be alive today." A small hint of anger towards himself was heard in his voice.

"Honey…" Katherine said slowly. "You can't hold yourself accountable for the actions of evil men. You did exactly what was expected of you. You did what any man would have done in that situation. You tried your best to save her. And that's what you do. You're a savior, baby. You ran into a burning house to save a man you barely know. You risked your life to save his. It's who you are. I know that what happened to you was the most horrible thing that could happen to anyone. But it made you who you are today. And I am grateful for the man you are. I need you. Sarah needs you. And to be honest, this town needs you… just the way you are." And even with all the pain and sorrow still welled up inside, the comfort of the words his wife said to him brought ease to his troubled mind. And so, they stood there and watched the storm. It was not long before he wrapped an arm around his wife and kissed her on the forehead and spoke the only words that truly matter to anyone.

"I love you."

By mid-afternoon of the following day, the streets were all but dried up. The sun was shining and only a few puffy white clouds drifted on the bright blue canvas. James and Jared were walking up one side of the street as they would normally do. This was something they did so that their presence would be seen, and if there was a problem they were easy to find. The two of them were carrying on a non — sensical conversation when James had abruptly stopped talking. His pace quickened and his hand reached down for his pistol. He came to a quick stop behind a man who had just gotten off his horse and was fixing something with the saddle. He was a man of an average and portly build. His scruffy hair showed signs of not being washed for a while. The life of a vagrant as it were. He and his men were noted for petty crimes. They were not much on the list of killers and really dangerous men. They seemed to only go after people that could afford it and even then, they never inflicted harm. As the man turned around, James drew his gun and had his arm fully extended with the barrel of his pistol only a fraction of an inch away from the center of the man's forehead. Then James spoke with a firmness deep in his voice.

"I know who you are Dirty Bill. And I know that you have not been to this town before. So, listen up because I am only going to say this once. You and your men are welcome in this town so long as you follow the rules here."

"Rules!?" Dirty Bill replied sarcastically.

"Yes, rules," James replied without changing his tone. "Rule number one. You and your men *will* hand over your firearms. All of them. They will be tagged and locked up until you are ready to leave. Rule number two. You and your men *will* respect this town and its citizens. If I get word of any trouble… if I hear a whisper… if a little bird lands on my windowsill, if I get a tingling in one of the tiny hairs on the back of my neck that has your name on it, so help me I will lock you up and ship you off to the governor who will try you and he *will* hang you."

"And if we don't?"

"Then you have two choices. You can either get back on your horses and ride straight out of this town—"

"Or?" Dirty Bill interrupted.

"Or I can pull this trigger right now and we can find out once and for all if you really do have shit for brains." There was not even a trace of joviality in James' voice as he spoke.

After a moment of silence, Dirty Bill erupted in a burst of laughter.

"I like you, Sheriff. You got balls," he said through that laughter. "All right boys. Hand 'em over. You won't be needin' 'em here."

As they handed over their weapons, James spoke up one last time.

"Thank you. And welcome to Dry River."

As Dirty Bill turned to walk towards the saloon, he gave the sheriff a slap on the shoulder and smiled. It was nice to have a place that they could unwind without hassle. James turned to his deputy.

"Make sure you tag these and lock 'em up."

"Will do, Sheriff." After a moment he added, "Not to impugn your fine judge of character, but do you think it is wise to allow men like Dirty Bill to have free rein in this town?"

"Absolutely. It all but guarantees we won't have an issue."

"I don't follow."

"You see, by allowing them to have freedom in this town, they now have a sense of respite. And for people who don't have a home, they can't afford to shoot down an opportunity like this."

"And if they do?"

"Then I will see that they are hung out to dry. So, you are going to keep your ears open, and your eyes peeled."

They headed back to the jailhouse and locked up Dirty Bill's weapons. James stayed there at his desk while Jared went back out into the streets just in case Dirty Bill and his men were to step out of line. A few hours had passed before Jared made his way back into the saloon to check on his quarry. Everyone was behaving. The piano music filled the room and laughter and multiple conversations added to the ambiance. Most were drinking as a few waitresses moseyed around delivering drinks. Jared's eyes scanned the place and the patrons within the saloon. After looking over those at the bar, he looked over the tables. At once, his eyes became transfixed on a man underneath a black hat. This was someone whom he had not seen before. And it was not one of Dirty Bill's men. As he moved closer, he got a better look at the man. His hair was long and mildly wavy. He had brown eyes and was athletically built. He had a trimly cut goatee and well-worn clothes. The most important thing that Jared noticed was a holster that still held a pistol within it. As he looked on, he soon recognized the man from posters and newspaper articles. It was none other than the Desert Fox. Knowing this really concerned Jared because this was a man not to be trifled with. Nevertheless, he had a job to do. He walked over to confront the patron.

"Um… excuse me, sir." As Jared spoke, he tried to mask the intimidation he felt. "Sir, I am going to have to ask… you for your gun." Try as he may, there was definitely some fear in his voice as he spoke. The Desert Fox said nothing and maintained his focus on the poker game. "Sir…you can't have a gun within the town limits." Again, the Desert Fox did not shift his head in the slightest. However, this time he spoke with a deep voice.

"I'm playing a game at the moment. Leave me alone."

Jared slowly reached for his pistol in an attempt to gain control of the situation. Again, the Desert Fox spoke up. This time with definite assurance in his voice.

"You really don't want to do that." Jared's hand froze in mid-motion. "Now run along."

Jared did just that. He left the saloon and headed straight to the jail. As he closed the door behind him, James looked up.

"We have a problem, Jimmy."

"Hah… Bill?". There was a hint of disappointment in his voice at the prospect that he misjudged Dirty Bill and his men.

"No… worse." Jared recounted, still exhibiting a tinge of fear in his voice. "Um… The Desert Fox is… ah…" After a deep exhale, he finished the statement. "He's sitting in our saloon." James shook his head.

"What is this? Infamous villains' day?" James got up and strapped on his holster. After checking that his revolver was fully loaded, he slid it back into the holster and made his way to the saloon with Jared close behind. As they emerged through the louvered wooden doors, Jared pointed him out. James walked over and stood behind and slightly to the right of the Desert Fox who was engaged in a five-card poker game. He slowly turned his head enough to get a glimpse of the sheriff's holster. With barely a move of his head, he then moved his head up for a quick gander of the sheriff's face before returning his focus to the cards he held in his hand.

"I'll take one," he said slowly as he tossed a card face down.

"I'm afraid I am going to have to ask you for your pistol, sir."

"Ten dollars," said Jack from across the table. Jack was a surly man with ragged hair, and he was missing a tooth from one too many bar fights.

"Make it twenty," the Desert Fox countered. He turned his head slightly towards James. "I can't do that, Sheriff."

"I see your twenty and raise you ten more," Jack responded.

"I wasn't asking you, sir," James stated firmly. At this point, a very stunning brunette walked over and leaned over the Desert Fox. She had tight curly hair that came well past her shoulders. Her eyes were a lighter shade of brown and her body was in great shape. In a pouting, albeit sexy voice she spoke up.

"You said you were gonna buy me a drink and spend some time with me."

The Desert Fox shifted his head slightly in a display of mild irritation.

"What the hell?" he said in his low and somber voice. "I get him on one side nagging about my pistol and now you on the other side nagging as well. I'm in the middle of a hand here. I'll be over later." He grabbed a stack of money. "Make it sixty."

The woman, who was now infuriated with his arrogance and lack of empathy, angrily responded.

"Good luck with your pair of threes!" With that, she turned and walked back to the bar in a huff. The Desert Fox lowered his head and shook it slightly in disbelief.

"Women," he muttered.

Jack started to laugh. He knew he had the hand now. All that money was his. With a happy grin, he declared his new bet.

"I'm all in." He grabbed the rest of the cash sitting in front of him. "That's two hundred and seventy dollars to you."

He finished the sentence with a chuckle. At this point, the Desert Fox stopped moving his head. After a slight pause, he looked up with a grin of his own.

He responded pleasantly to Jack, "I call."

He turned over his cards and stated his hand. "Straight flush."

At the sight of his loss, Jack was furious.

"You fucking bastard! She said you had a pair of threes!" Jack shouted as he slammed his fists on the table. As he pushed himself up, James reached for his gun. "You're a goddamned cheater!" James drew his gun and pointed it at Jack.

"Sit down, Jack. He didn't cheat."

"The hell he didn't."

"How many cards did he draw?"

"One."

"That's right... one card." James calmly explained. "How many times have you drawn only one card when you only had a pair? What he did might be considered unethical, but he did not cheat."

James now changed his focus. He turned the gun towards the Desert Fox.

"Now, I asked nicely before, but now I am demanding it. Hand over your pistol."

The Desert Fox made a very slow move and used only his elbow to lift back his long trench coat to reveal the handle of the pistol that resided within his holster. When James saw that inlaid ivory handle with a wolf's head carving, he lost it. For it was the same handle as the pistol in James' hand which meant only one thing.

"You son of a bitch!" James exclaimed as he struck the Desert Fox on the back of the neck, rendering him unconscious. The entire saloon fell silent because they had never seen their sheriff show such a display that was clearly out of character. "Jared, take this piece of trash to the jail and lock him up."

James undid the holster around the Desert Fox's waist and then proceeded to gather up the money on the table. He then walked out of the saloon and headed to the jail. Jared was just closing the cell door when James walked in. Jared handed over the cell door key and James made his way to the cell. As he unlocked the door, he uttered a request.

"You should leave, Jared," he said in a very dark voice. "It would be best if you were not here for this." James opened the cell door and walked through it.

"For what?" Jared asked with a concerned intonation.

"Just leave! NOW!" James stated in a terrifyingly shaky voice. Jared too was concerned by James' shift in behavior, and he left quickly. James shut the cell door and stood there holding the second pistol in his hand. The Desert Fox slowly came to and began rubbing the back of his head.

"Man... you didn't have to hit me," he said calmly.

"SHUT UP!" James forcibly stated. The Desert Fox stood up and started to turn around when James ordered him to stop. "Don't you *dare* turn around." James raised the pistol and slowly cocked the hammer.

"You going to shoot me in the back while I'm locked up in a cell?" The Desert Fox's tone never changed. He still remained calm as he spoke.

"That depends on your answer to this next question." James paused for only a moment before continuing. "Where did you get this pistol from?"

As the Desert Fox answered, Katherine came in with Jared behind her.

"I got it from a dead man."

"James! What are you thinking?!" Katherine exclaimed.

"Go home, Katherine. This does not concern you," James ordered.

"Go home why? So you can commit murder?"

"He committed murder first. This is the asshole that killed my brother!"

Katherine stepped back.

"What?" she asked shocked.

"You got the wrong asshole, Jimmy," the Desert Fox stated with assurance, "and if you don't put that gun down you are going to become the asshole you were looking for. Because you will be the one to kill your brother."

"Bullshit!" James countered incredulously.

Slowly, the Desert Fox turned around.

"When you were seven you fell out of a tree, and I carried you over a mile. When we were almost home, you begged me to put you down so that Mom wouldn't see and be worried." A look that could not be described came over James' face. He opened his hand on the grip and the pistol rolled forward on his trigger finger. It dangled there for a moment before it slid off and fell to the floor. As it landed, the pistol discharged a shot that broke the silence. Katherine screamed as the bullet lodged itself in the desk.

"Jesus!" the Desert Fox remarked.

James lowered himself to the floor. His breathing became heavy and labored. He could not move. From his reaction, Katherine knew it to be true as well, but her shock kept her from being able to move as well.

"Um... can you let us out, Jimmy?" Eric asked. He moved over and helped his brother to his feet. The door slid partially open and was assisted by Jared who opened it the rest of the way. As James and Eric stood there in silence, they stared intently at each other. This was broken by one of the most heartfelt embraces ever given. They were both in tears.

"I... thou-thought y-you were de-dead," James managed.

"As did I," Eric replied. As the embrace ended, James wiped away the remaining tears. Through a sniffle, he introduced his deputy Jared and his wife Katherine to his brother.

"Let's go home," Katherine said somberly, "I know someone else who would like to meet him."

The emotional air was so thick it was all but visible. Eric moved over to the desk and picked up his holster. As he started to put it on, Jared spoke up.

"Um... James," he said, "he may be your brother, but the law is the law. He can't carry those here."

James shook his head.

"You're right Jared," he remarked. With that, he walked over to the desk.

"You're kidding right, Jimmy?" Eric countered.

"Nope," James stated firmly, "it is the law here."

He pulled out a small and circular object and tossed it to his brother. "Only the law can carry guns in town."

Eric glanced down at the object he caught. It clearly stated the simple word: DEPUTY on it.

"Well, I guess now he can carry them," Jared said with a smile.

As James, Eric and Katherine made their way to his house, Jared remained out on the streets and patrolled as usual. Back at the house, James and Eric were sitting at the table with a bottle of whiskey and two glasses. Katherine came around the corner with a bundle in her arm.

"And this is Sarah," she said with a smile. She carefully handed the little one over to Eric.

"She is adorable," Eric responded. As Sarah smiled and cooed at him, a smile breached his lips. This was because he never thought a day like this would come. He interacted with Sarah for a few minutes.

As Katherine took her back, she looked at her husband.

"I'm going to go lay her down." she said. She then made her way out of the room.

"Sorry I hit you in the back of the head," James said apologetically.

"It's all good."

"It's just that when I saw that pistol, I could only think of that day."

"I can understand."

"I guess I should tell you that I also buried you," James said with a light-hearted smile as he took a drink from his glass.

"You buried me?" Eric asked rhetorically.

"When I came to in the morning, Mom and Dad were dead. I called and called for you but never got a response. So, after digging a hole for mom and dad, I dug one for you as well. After I was finished, I went inside and grabbed Dad's holster and pistol. I left with no care of where I would end up. Truth is, I really didn't care where I ended up. Mainly because I buried my own heart there with you all that day. I wished I would just die. I finally collapsed. The next thing I knew, I was waking up to Katie wiping my forehead with a cloth. Her parents raised me from then on. They enrolled me into the school where I met Jared."

"He kicked Jared's ass that day," Katherine pleasantly interjected.

"Really?" Eric questioned.

"Hehe… yeah. After all I'd been through, he made a crack about mom. I lost it." James continued his recounting of what happened. "But we became friends after that. When I finished school, my father—in—law gave me a job at his bank. I was later offered a job as a deputy which obviously I took. And in time I became sheriff. I married Katie and we had Sarah. Life has been good for us. And then, I find you."

"Mom would be so proud of you," Eric said. "I can't believe how well you turned out," he added with admiration.

"Well, I guess God wasn't finished with me back then. What about you?"

"I don't think that Mom would be too proud of my life." Eric took a drink before continuing. "Father maybe, but not Mother."

"Considering the circumstances, I think she would understand," James added comfortingly.

"Maybe."

"How did you manage to get away anyhow?" James asked. He was anxious to learn his brother's story.

"Well, I tried to lead them away from the house. As I ran through the forest, I tripped over a root or a rock or something. The man chasing me thought it was his shot that took me down and he went away. I don't know how long I was down there, but it was still dark when I came around. I made my way back to the house. When I saw you and mom lying there, I lost it. I left in a rage, and I was full of the desire to avenge your deaths. I took all the guns from the other two dead men outside. I then made my way to the river, crossing it, I continued on my way. Before dawn, I came to a town. I snuck into the first house I could and stole some food. When I came out, I noticed a stable with a few horses. One of those horses was just *begging* to come with me. So, I obliged, and we rode off together. I found another safe place to stop and eat and rest. When I woke, it was all but nightfall again. I got up and continued on my journey. Next thing I knew, I found myself at the edge of the desert. It was chilly, but the full moon's light illuminated the landscape almost like the sun. I found a hideout and with a little work, it became the perfect place. It's virtually invisible unless you know what to look for. So that became my new home. I would ride from there into neighboring towns and gather provisions in whatever way I could. I continued to work on the draw. I wanted to be faster than Father ever was. As I got older, I got some chances to play poker and make some money. In doing so, I made some rather interesting friends. I would ride with different vagrants when I needed extra money. And it worked out in my favor. By doing so, I was able to find out who was responsible for Mother and Father's death. It was the Three Brother's Gang. Apparently, Father was a part of the gang before he met Mother."

"Father was an outlaw?" James blurted out.

"Apparently so. He even planned one of their largest heists. They managed not to get caught. At least not until after father left the gang. They were ambushed and several gang members were arrested and brought up on trial. The two brothers managed to bribe the jailer to release their brethren. Then they planned on retribution because they believed that father set them up."

"Do you think he did?" James inquired.

"From what I know of Father and from what I heard I don't think so. But they believed it and when they finally found him, they went to get their revenge."

"That's why they came that night." James filled the glasses again as he spoke.

"Yes. Later, when they believed we were all dead, some of the remaining members began to brag about that night and how nobody would ever cross their gang again. I found this out over time through others who knew the gang. Naturally, since they believed I was dead, it was fairly easy to get close to them. After the first batch started dying, they caught on that it was me. Because I was able to disappear in the desert, I got the colorful moniker of the Desert Fox. I kind of like it."

"It's catchy," James commented. They clinked glasses and downed the drinks. James topped them off one more time.

"Thanks."

"Don't mention it."

After another sip, Eric continued with his recounting of events.

"It all worked out and I kept searching for the last brother. He was there that night. He's the one you shot. From what I heard, you got him in the shoulder pretty well. The downside to my taking them out is that for every gang member I kill, two more take his place. But truthfully, I could care less. Once I kill the last brother, I'm hanging up the name and I am going to disappear from that life just like Father did."

"Do you think he is here?" Katherine asked, "Is that why you came to Dry River?"

"Well, I first heard that there was a man here with a unique silver pistol with an inlaid ivory handle, just like mine. So, naturally, like you, my first thought was yes. But when I learned that the man was the sheriff here, that made no sense. I had to come and see for myself. When I got to the saloon, I asked the bartender what the sheriff's name was. When he told me, I could not believe it. So, I waited for you. When your deputy arrived, I had to get him to bring you along. I will admit that my original plan was to kill you and take back Father's pistol. But, when I saw your face, I knew you really were my brother."

"You did?"

"You look like Mother. And I could definitely see traces of Father too. And it's a good thing that I like to see the face of whomever I kill."

"I say. So, I guess… thank you for not killing me!" James said with a smile as he hoisted his glass.

"Likewise," Eric said, doing the same. They clinked glasses, tapped them on the table and downed the contents.

Katherine made a very special dinner that night. They all enjoyed the wonderful meal and conversation. That night, after Sarah was put to bed, James and Eric sat out on the front porch with more whiskey in their glasses.

"So, you made a home here I see," Eric said proudly. "It's a very nice town."

"Yeah. This is a wonderful town. The people are really nice, and we really don't have too much trouble here."

"You got a nice family too." There was a twinge of jealousy in Eric's voice. A family of his own was something that he never thought would be possible. Even though he was as fast as he was, there was still a part of him that really believed he would die before he ever had the chance to have a family.

"I got lucky there. Katie and Sarah are amazing. Despite everything, I guess God worked it all out. Even better now that you are here."

"Truth is, Jimmy, I gave up on Jesus a long time ago. After everything that He took from me, I felt He was no better than Satan himself. If He truly cared, Mom and Dad would still be alive."

"Well, after all that we have been through, I can understand why. But trust me, He ain't done with you just yet."

"Somehow I doubt it."

"He brought us back together," James said with certainty.

"Well, there is that."

"Believe me, I was about to give up on Him too. But when I look back, I see that, even with as bad as it was, He never left me. And He hasn't left you either."

"Well, if He was or is there, I never knew it."

They sat there enjoying the cool night air. James changed the pace of the conversation.

"So, who was the woman in the saloon with you?"

"That's Elena. I met her near the border about a year ago now. Over time I've grown to trust her. Maybe if I live through this, I'll be as lucky as you."

"It's possible."

"Here's hoping."

"Where do you see yourself when you've seen this through?"

"If I succeed, I'm not sure. Never truly thought about it."

"Well, just so you know. That badge I tossed you wasn't just for the hell of it. It's an offer if you want it. The job's always open to you."

"Wow," Eric said as he looked back down at the badge on his lapel. "I never had a real job before."

"Well, like me, you were born for this. But there is a catch."

"Oh yeah?" Eric inquired.

"Yeah." James took a sip before enunciating the catch. "You have to live here in Dry River."

Eric raised his glass and spoke just before taking a drink.

"I think I could handle that. And maybe Elena too."

As they finished their whiskeys, James' expression turned serious.

"So, I have one question that you *didn't* ask."

"And I won't ask that one. You have a nice family here. A nice life here. I would not dare ask that of you."

"But you know you don't have to go at it alone, Eric."

"Look, there's only one more left. I'll take care of him and then I'll return to take you up on your offer. But for now, it's time for bed."

"Okay, I'll see you in the morning."

James and Eric went back inside. Katherine had the couch all made up for Eric to sleep on.

Back in the bedroom, James was sitting up on his side with his feet on the floor. Katherine rolled over onto her side. Her body cradled around his and she rested her head on her hand. Looking up at him with a sympathetic gaze, she could tell something was off.

"Penny for your thoughts, my love?" she asked quietly.

"Seeing my brother today, and hearing about what he did and how he never stopped fighting to avenge our parents makes me feel as though I failed. If it wasn't me who killed my mother, I still failed them by not avenging their deaths as Eric has done."

"Jimmy..." Katherine said soothingly, "you know that vengeance is blind. Do you remember me telling you that you did exactly as the Lord planned for you to do?"

"Yeah..." James responded slowly.

"Perhaps the reason you were not filled with such vengeance was that He knew your brother was still alive and would be more capable of taking care of it. And you, you were kept out of it so that you could be his respite when all was done."

James thought about what she said. It seemed as though it was a plan that was predestined to be. Her words rang true. He laid down and she curled up under his arm. With a soft kiss on the forehead, they closed their eyes and drifted off to sleep.

As the morning came, so did a knock at the door. James opened it to see a young boy of twelve standing there.

"Can I help you?" James inquired.

"I'm looking for the Desert Fox," the young boy responded.

"What for?"

"I have a message for him." James invited the little messenger in as Eric came around the corner.

"You have something for me?" Eric asked.

"They found the last brother. Here's where he's stayin'," the boy answered as he handed over a folded piece of paper. Eric, in turn, tossed the boy a few dollars as compensation for the delivery.

"Thank you," Eric added.

The boy nodded and left.

"Kinda young for a spy, isn't he?" James asked jovially.

"Not at all, Jimmy," Eric slyly remarked, "they make the best spies because they are the least suspected.

And some, like this one, have a knack for gathering information."

After looking at the paper, Eric mentioned that the last brother was closer than he thought.

"Eric, I had a thought last night."

"What is it, Jimmy?"

"Instead of killing him, maybe we should arrest him and let him stand trial. The governor can kill him, and we can be free of this nightmare."

"But this man killed our mother, Jimmy," Eric said with disdain. "I can't just hand him over."

"You can. And you know as well as me that this is the better way to deal with this."

"I don't think I can. If I see him, I'm going to want to kill him."

"I have faith in you, brother," James said confidently, "and I will be there with you."

"You're coming with me?"

"If we handle it my way, then yes. Please, this is my chance to avenge Mother's death as well but not subvert my own morality."

Eric pondered it for a moment. And, just as before, there was nothing he would not do for his brother. A smile came over his face as he spoke.

"Okay, Jimmy. For you, we will do it your way."

After breakfast, James and Eric mounted their horses and rode out of town. It was a little more than a day's ride from Dry River to their destination. So, as night began to fall, they stopped and set up a small camp for the night. They sat by the fire trading stories and spent more time catching up. And when morning came, they were up on their way again. By mid-morning, they arrived at a small house in an isolated location. James and Eric walked up to the front door and knocked. There was no response.

"You think we should knock again?" James asked.

"Allow me," Eric said as he stepped back and raised his foot. With a simple thrust forward, the door gave way. "Uh-oh, I think I knocked a little too hard."

"I hate when that happens."

After a slight simultaneous chuckle, they cautiously entered the seemingly abandoned place. The place was in a state of disarray. It appeared as though the house had not been cleaned for several months. Flies were buzzing around a plate of food that, although it was not rotten, looked like it was well on its way there.

It was not long before an older man came around the corner waving a pistol and shouting, "Get the hell out of my house!"

Before he could bring his pistol into range and bear on the target of one of the two would-be intruders, Eric drew his and fired. The shot rang through the old man's gun and his hand as well. The old man winced as he grabbed the newly injured hand.

"Goddammit!" he screamed.

"You're under arrest, for the murder of John and Anna Harper, and for several bank and train heists!"

James stated with authority. Eric grabbed the old man forcibly. As they were leaving, a woman called out.

"What's going on?" she asked, "where are you taking him?"

"To Dry River and then to the governor to stand trial for murder and robbery," James answered. And on that note, they exited the place and mounted their horses. Because there were only two horses, Eric tied a rope around the man's handcuffed hands like a leash so he could not run away. In James and Eric's eyes, it was fair treatment for this scumbag. This time, as night fell, Eric and James rolled out their makeshift beds near the fire. To make sure their captive did not escape, James loosened one of the handcuffs for a moment. To make sure their captive did not escape, James drew his weapon and then loosened one of the handcuffs for a moment.

"Wrap your arms around the tree." He obliged, and James cuffed him there.

"How the hell am I supposed to sleep like this?" the man asked incredulously.

James leaned in close to him.

"I really don't give a damn if you sleep at all.," James whispered with fierce anger lacing the quietness of his response. "That's not my problem." With that, he turned and went back to the fire and his brother. They sat there for a while enjoying the warmth. At one point Eric rose and made his way to the tree. He squatted down with his pistol drawn. He waved it slightly from side to side as he spoke.

"You know, you really should thank my brother. I wanted to kill you but he convinced me otherwise. I bet you don't remember either of us. You see, twenty-six years ago, you and some of your *friends* paid us a visit. You killed our parents. You, in particular, *you* killed my mother. That one… that one over there? He gave you that nice little reminder on your shoulder. I have been searching for you for some time now. I killed the others and… *GOD!* I wanted to kill you. But I promised my brother that I wouldn't. Unless you give me a reason to. And I *really* hope that you give me a reason to on this trip. *PLEASE* give me a reason." Eric paused for a moment, waiting for a response. But the old man did not speak. "No? No reason? Maybe you're not as dumb as you look. But no matter, you *will* die."

With that, Eric rose to his feet and made his way back to the warmth of the fire.

With the walking prisoner in tow, it took longer to make the return trip. But, by late afternoon, the three of them were back in Dry River. The old man was placed in a cell. James and Eric sat down.

"You know, I really wanted the satisfaction of killing him myself. But I must say, I am enjoying this aspect of it. Let him suffer for a while," Eric commented.

"See…" James returned, "sometimes it is better to wait than to just kill right away."

"I never thought about that before, but now I see the pleasure in it." As they sat there savoring the moment, a small commotion arose just outside the door.

"Now what?" James muttered as he rose. Eric followed his brother to the door. They opened to door to find a small group of men outside. The one in front had a striking resemblance to the individual that was perched on a cot behind about a hundred and twenty square feet of wrought iron bars.

"I've come for my father!" the man in front called out. His name was David. He was of average build and had scraggly hair. His face was muffled by a small coat of fur that was on the way to becoming a full-fledged beard. He seemed to be about four years younger than James.

"Your father is held for murder. He'll stand trial before the governor in a few days. You can come for him then," James replied sternly.

"Or I can just shoot you now and take him," David said aggressively.

Eric drew his pistol and had it trained on David's forehead before he could blink.

"I don't think even *you* could be that stupid, Dave," Eric countered. "He *will* stand trial and the law will decide his fate."

"You want a war, Sheriff?" David exclaimed. "You'll get one! Mark my words!"

He turned to his men and shifted his head in a motion to announce that they were leaving. They turned their horses around and rode off into the night.

"Better stay on our toes tonight," Eric suggested.

"I think we should take shifts tonight and watch this bastard. Just in case they try to come for him," James added.

"Agreed," Eric and Jared confirmed in unison.

"I guess that means we get no sleep tonight," Jared remarked.

"The perks of the job," James said sarcastically.

There was a simultaneous sarcastic nod from both Eric and Jared. James went home to let Katherine know that he would not be back that night. He then returned outside to where Eric and Jared were waiting.

"So, his transport will be here in the morning?" Jared inquired.

"Yup," James answered, "we just gotta keep him there till then. So, make sure you stay alert."

James took the first watch. Eric and Jared started their evening patrols. They still had a town to watch over, so they made periodic rounds in the saloon and on the streets. Nothing eventful happened. It came time for the second watch. Jared took on that responsibility. The night air was calm. A gentle breeze softly filled the town. Eric looked up at the blackness above them.

"A lot of stars out tonight, huh?" James remarked.

This is nothing," Eric replied, "you should see the night sky in the desert. Now *that's* a lot of stars."

"Never been that far out," James said.

"Well, maybe when we're done with this, we'll take a ride out there."

"That sounds like a plan." They passed by the saloon again. While they were making that round, a group of five men came out of the darkness. They had been lying in wait, watching for them for the last few hours. Now they had their chance. They stood outside James' house and unleashed a fury of bullets. The shots echoed through the street as the bullets tore through the house. Katherine and Elena managed to keep themselves and Sarah safe as they took cover. From the saloon, people shouted for the sheriff. James and Eric came running out. They did not stop when they passed the louvered saloon doors. Their pistols were already drawn before they even reached that point. As they hit the street, they ran towards the rampage. As soon as the group was in sight, James and Eric began firing while they ran. The four pistols they held were enough to at least startle the group. The five men turned their horses and rode off in the opposite direction. As they reached the house, James could hear Sarah screaming. He ran faster than he ever thought he could. He shouted for his wife as he busted through the bullet-ridden door. Eric stayed out on the porch with a very vigilant eye. Jared came running up the street and was soon in view of those in the battered house.

"Jimmy!" Katherine called out as she came out of a back room. Tears were streaming heavily down her face as she cradled Sarah and tried to calm her down. Elena followed close behind. "We're okay honey. We're okay." James reached out and took Sarah in his arms. He held her so close one could not tell that she was not a permanent part of his body.

"Shhh… shhh… there, there now," James said softly, "it's okay, Princess. Everything's okay." He slowly bounced her on his arm as his other hand lovingly caressed her back in a gentle rubbing motion. Eric and Jared entered the house. Elena ran to Eric and threw her arms around him.

"What the hell happened?" Jared asked.

"Those bastards shot up my house."

"Is everyone okay?"

"Yes," James responded. His efforts to calm down his daughter were working. "Thank God." As this was going on, the real plan unfolded over at the jail. Another group of men were watching the jail to see when Jared would leave. As soon as that happened, they lashed two ropes around the window bars and tied the ends to the two horses. They gave a few shouts to encourage the horses pulled in short bursts. It did not take long for the wall to give way. With this newly created point of egress, the old man climbed out from his cell. There was a horse without a rider just waiting for him to hop up on. They cut the ropes that held the former window and then they rode off into the night.

Back at the house, everything began to settle down. Katherine took Sarah back to her bed as the others remained near the front door. The realization of the chain of events hit James and Eric at the same time. Like a speeding train. With only a glance at each other, they rushed to the door.

"Stay here!" James shouted as an order to Jared.

As they sprinted down the street, Eric called out, "Are you thinking what I'm thinking?"

"Yes!" James responded.

When they burst through the front door of the sheriff's office, they could see the hole in the back wall.

"My house was a distraction to get us away from the jail so they could get him out."

As they looked around, fury and anger welled up from deep within James' soul. The same feelings rose deep within Eric. With a very deep and long-suppressed rage and heartfelt shout, James flipped his desk. After a few moments of heavy breathing, he looked back at the hole in the wall. "They've gone too far. This time they crossed the line."

"So, what do you want to do?" Eric inquired. Deep inside he felt he already knew the answer, but it was important for him to hear it out loud. As the memory of both his own house and wife and daughter as well as when he was only eight years old, there was only one response to give.

"Kill 'em all, Eric. Kill 'em all." There was a deep ferocity and solid determination in his voice as he spoke those words. There was nothing more they could accomplish there and so they made their way back to

James' house. Sarah was asleep and Katherine, Jared and Elena had cleaned up most of the mess. As James entered the house, Katherine ran to her husband and embraced him. It was so deep an embrace that she could have squeezed the life out of him. There was a clear display within her eyes that she was immensely grateful that she could still hold him. When the embrace finally reached its climax and subsequent ending, they looked deep into each other's eyes. Before he even said a single word, she knew every one of the thousand thoughts racing through his mind. And she agreed with every single one of them.

"Katie... Eric and I have to leave," he stated firmly. "We have to end this once and for all. If we don't, I may not be able to protect you and Sarah. And I will not let the same thing happen to her that happened to my parents."

"I know Jimmy..." she said softly, "I know you have to go." Tears welled up inside and hid behind her eyes.

"I will come home, baby. I will come home," he said. "I love you, Katherine."

James then slowly walked into the room where his little princess was fast asleep. The beauty of seeing her little body sprawled out filled his heart deeply. He leaned down as she slowly opened her eyes and looked up at him.

"Are the bad men gone, Daddy?" she asked softly.

"They are, for now, Princess," James responded. "But your uncle Eric and I are going to make sure that they never return again." She smiled gently at this. James leaned down and gave her a soft unicorn kiss on her forehead.

"Give me another," she asked with such sweet innocence. James happily obliged. She reached up and wrapped her little arms around him. Even though it was only a short embrace, to James it felt like it lasted an eternity. And there was not a single thing wrong with that. Soon, her arms slid off from her father and she lay back down. James gave her one more unicorn kiss.

"I love you, Princess."

"I love you too, Daddy."

He walked back out into the living room. From the bookshelf James took up his mother's Bible. He turned around and knelt down on the floor. With the Bible cradled in his hand, he bowed his head and offered up a silent prayer that he would live to see this through till the end. Eric came over and knelt down beside his brother. He placed a hand on James' shoulder and bowed his own head. James looked up slightly and saw that it was his brother. He smiled and lowered his head again.

"Lord, forgive us for what we are about to do. I understand that it is wrong in Your eyes, but for the safety of my family, I have no choice. We must undertake this task. So, we ask that you watch over us as we proceed with this venture. And we ask that you keep our family safe. But in all, Your will be done. Amen."

"Amen," Eric echoed softly. James replaced the Bible on the shelf. Then he turned to Jared.

"Stay here and keep the town in order." He pulled off his badge and tossed it to Jared. "You're the sheriff now, Jared. At least until I return."

"Understood, Jimmy," Jared answered, pinning the badge to his lapel. They sealed the agreement with a solid handshake. James turned back to his wife, and they gave each other the most passionate of embraces. An embrace that could rival any embrace ever shared by anyone in the history of all humankind.

"I love you," James whispered in her ear.

"I love you too," Katherine returned. When they separated, she turned to Eric and gave him a hug as well. While in his arms she softly whispered to him as well. "Please bring my husband home." And her plea did not fall on deaf ears.

"I will," Eric responded. Their embrace did not last nearly as long as her previous embrace. When it was finished, James and Eric walked to the front door. Elena came over and gave Eric a kiss and a hug as well. But no words were exchanged. As they went through the front door, James turned back to look at his wife.

"I love you," he said one last time.

She let him know the same and with that he closed the door behind them. Katherine turned her head away from the door as tears filled her eyes and burst from their constraints.

Outside, James and Eric were confronted by three men who were familiar to James. As they sat amongst their horses, one of them looked down at James.

"We heard what happened, what they did to your wife and daughter. And that is just not right." It was Dirty Bill and the men who rode into town with him. "So, if you would be so kind as to return our weapons so we can come with you?"

"Dirty Bill, this is not your fight," James pointed out. "I can't ask you to come on board."

"Fair enough," Dirty Bill relented, "you said we could have our guns back when we were ready to leave town. Well, we're ready to leave in whatever direction you are headed. And it's just Bill."

After a moment he continued, "I never really liked that damned moniker."

"Thank you, Bill."

Bill introduced the two men behind him.

"This here is Chris, and the other fella is Kirk." Chris was the tallest of the trio at about five-ten. He had hair that was full of tight curls and scruffy beard growth. He looked to be of either Spanish or Italian descent. As for Kirk, he stood only about five foot six and was all but bald on top. He was clearly of American descent. James pointed to the man next to him.

"This is my brother, Eric," he stated.

Chris looked down from his horse as he recognized Eric.

"You th' Desert Fox? Ain'tcha?" Chris remarked.

"Like Bill said, I'm just Eric tonight."

"Fair enough," Chris said.

"Now..." James said, "let's go get your guns."

They made their way back to the jail where James unlocked the cabinet and pulled out their weapons. As Bill and his companions were wrapping their holsters around their waists, James and Eric stocked up on ammo and grabbed the rifles that were in a separate cabinet. As they finished, James turned to the rest of the men before him.

"I will make this one point very clear. We are going after members of the Three Brothers Gang *only*. Do not kill any other men. If you do, you will be next. Is that understood?"

"You got it," Bill responded. Chris answered similarly.

"What if they draw down on us?" Kirk inquired.

"Shoot to maim only," Eric answered.

"Exactly," James stated firmly, "we are not out on a free-for-all. This is a personal score, and I will not inflate collateral damage if I can avoid it." Kirk nodded to show he understood. After loading the last shot into his rifle, James tipped it up.

"Let's ride!" he ordered.

As they departed from the jail and entered the street to mount their horses, citizens of the town saw these determined men and knew that they did not want anything to do with the Three Brothers tonight because a reckoning that would make hell look like a summer camp was about to descend on them. James and Eric and the others rode around to the back of the jail where the window with the bars and rope that was still attached lay on the ground. Eric hopped down off his horse and walked around in a pattern to look for evidence. Within moments, he pinpointed their direction and climbed back onto his horse and led the way. Several times he would stop and climb down. Repeating a similar process, he would look for signs that would tell him where to head next. His tracking skills were remarkable, and he was completely in tune with his surroundings.

The trail led them to a town that was about two days' ride south of Dry River. It would be like comparing night and day. This town was a haven for vagrants and degenerates. The exterior of the buildings was a disgrace. There were drunken men passed out in the street. One of them was having their pockets cleaned out by a young boy and nobody seemed to care. The saloon doubled as a brothel and the women paraded around advertising their goods. Truth be told though they were not top-notch women in the looks department. James told his brother and the others to wait outside as he went into the saloon. The inside of this pigsty was worse than the outside. A man lay in the corner and James could not tell if the man was passed out drunk or flat out dead. Of course, that determination meant nothing to him. James remained focused on his objective which was to find out if any of the members of the Three Brothers gang were there in the saloon or in the town. A scantily dressed woman approached James and tried to offer herself to him. James politely refused her offer and she moved on to find another potential prospect. He made his way to the bartender. After a short conversation, the bartender confirmed that there were three members of the gang upstairs enjoying themselves with some of the enterprising women. James thanked the bartender and flipped a few bills onto the counter as a secondary thank you. He made his way outside to inform the others.

"Eric… Bill, you two come with me," James commanded. "You two stay here and keep watch," he told Chris and Kirk. Eric and Bill dismounted their horses and followed James back inside the haven for degenerates. Chris looked over at Kirk.

"Stay here," he said, "I want to check something out."

"Sure…" Kirk agreed. "Make me the lone babysitter," he added jovially. Chris hopped down off his horse and headed off down the street. Back inside the saloon, James and Eric and Bill each stood outside three doors. Behind each of these doors was a member of the Three Brothers gang. They were intently wrapped up in the pleasurable company of the burlesque women they chose for the night. None of them knew the fate that awaited them on the other side of the door.

Simultaneously, the three doors swung open. Before the men could react, James and the others opened fire killing all three members. James walked up to the man that he just removed from the world and reached into his pocket. A moment later, he removed a stack of cash. He turned around and exited the room. Eric and Bill met him in the hall. They calmly walked down the stairs and as they passed the bar, James tossed the stack of money he just procured from the dead man upstairs onto the bar.

"For the mess," he stated coldly, and the three men exited the saloon. As they cleared the saloon entrance, Chris was just making it back to his horse.

"Where the hell did you go?" Bill angrily inquired. "This is no time for a stroll."

Chris looked over as he climbed back onto his horse.

"Actually, I found a few more members. They are camped a little over a mile east of here," Chris responded proudly.

"Nice job, Chris," Eric commented. They turned their horses and headed out of town in an easterly direction. They kept their distance but got close enough to confirm that the information was accurate. As they stood behind some cover, they spied on their quarry.

"So, what do we do? Ambush 'em now?" Kirk asked.

"No," Eric replied, "we wait 'til they are asleep and then we surprise them." He looked at his brother. "Let's have a little fun, shall we?" James nodded in agreement.

They climbed down from their horses and waited. One of them always made it a point to keep an eye on the men at the camp. While they waited for nightfall, Kirk knelt down beside Eric.

"So, you're the Desert Fox?" he said in admiration. "I can't believe it."

"What's so hard to believe?" Eric inquired. "After all, I'm just a man, you know."

"But I've heard many stories about you. About how fast you are. And how you can disappear. I just never thought I would have the privilege of riding with you."

"Well..." Eric smiled, "I wouldn't get too excited."

"Why not?"

"Because there's a very good chance, we aren't going to survive this and be able to tell anyone," Bill said as he walked by.

"Oh..." Kirk's voice trailed off.

"Hey..." Chris called out quietly to Kirk, "it's your turn to keep watch. Kirk rose and went to his post as temporary sentry. Finally, the time had come. It was late into the night as they huddled together. After a moment, they separated, and each went to a particular spot. Eric walked over to his brother. He pulled his pistols from their home in his holster and handed them over to James.

"You sure about this?" James asked as he tucked Eric's pistols into his own belt.

"Trust me, Jimmy," he responded with a smile. He then removed his coat and draped it over a branch nearby. With one final look at his brother, he walked off into the direction of the camp. He quietly moseyed past the sleeping bunch and knelt down at the edge of their fire and extended his hands to warm them up. He reached down and grabbed a stick and began to stoke the fire. It did not take long before one of the men woke up. Drawing his gun and pointing it in Eric's direction, he spoke up.

"Who the hell are you?"

"Just a traveler passing by," Eric responded, "saw your fire and figured it would be a nice place to warm my hands. Think you could hand me another log? It's getting kind of low."

There was no fear in Eric's voice. In fact, there was a sort of playfulness in his tone as he spoke. The other two men woke up.

"Who's this?!" one of them asked.

"Don't know. Says he's a traveler." The gun was still trained on the Desert Fox.

"Where's your guns?" the third man asked.

"They're right here," Eric said with certainty as he reached into the empty holster on his right side. He pulled out his hand with his forefinger and thumb extended in the shape of an imaginary pistol. This caused a chuckle among the men.

"What...?" Eric asked as he looked down at his imaginary pistol in an oblivious nature as if he could not fathom why they would be laughing. "You never saw a hand gun before?"

"You are one crazy fool," the man with the gun stated.

"Crazy?" Eric inquired. "Why? All you have to do is believe." He turned to the guy to his left. "Try it."

The man scoffed at him.

"No, really. Try it."

"Go ahead. We got 'im covered," the man with the gun confirmed. The man on the left followed suit with the Desert Fox and made an imaginary pistol with his hand.

"Very good. Oh, that's a very nice pistol. Looks expensive," Eric stated jovially. The men laughed at his insanity. "Now, point it over here at him. Go ahead." The man did so and was still chuckling at the incredulity of the situation. "Now... do you believe that you're holding a real pistol?"

"I guess... Yeah... Sure," the man agreed.

"Now, count to three and say *bang* as loud as you can." Eric goaded. "Ready? One... two... three." As he hit the third count, the man did as instructed to do.

"BANG!" he stated loudly. As he did, a real shot rang out as a bullet struck the man holding the gun in the head. He fell over immediately. Eric turned his imaginary pistol to the third man and nonchalantly said *bang* as another shot rang out and another bullet struck the third man and he fell to the ground.

"What the hell…?" the last man standing said in disbelief. Eric now trained his imaginary pistol on this last man.

"Don't even think of moving your hand," Eric commanded. The terrified man obliged. "I want to know where David is."

"Who?"

"Don't play dumb with me." Eric pushed. "Where's David?" The man did not speak. "Tell me or I'll say 'bang'. And if I do, you know what happens."

"Please… d-don't say it."

"Last time… where's David?"

"I don't know."

"Then you're of no use to me," Eric said slowly. He followed it up with one last word. "Bang!" A final shot rang out and the last man fell. As Eric walked back to the others, Kirk looked over at Chris.

"Told you he could get one of them to kill the other," Kirk said. After a moment, he continued. "Now, pay up." Chris pulled some money out and handed it over.

"Damn!" he stated in the process. They camped out for the night and in the morning, Eric resumed his tracking.

They continued riding east until they came to another town. They entered the town and spread out to inquire about other members of the Three Brothers

Gang. There were mixed reports of some members who lingered around but nobody could confirm that any were there at the present moment. The five men slipped into the local saloon for a drink to pass the time. This saloon was far nicer than the last one they had entered. However, law and order still seemed a little bit scarce. They took a table in the back of the saloon to discuss their plans. All of a sudden, a loud voice boomed over the noise in the saloon.

"I'm lookin' for the Desert Fox!" he called out. The saloon fell silent as Eric looked up.

"You've found him," Eric replied.

"You been huntin' down my friends and murdering them. Now, I'm here to return th' favor. Meet me in th' street now!" the man demanded. Without recourse, Eric rose from his seat. All eyes were on him as he made his way through the saloon. James and the others followed closely behind him. As they exited the saloon, a crowd began to form. The angry man stood there in the street waiting for him. James and Bill and the others remained on the porch of the saloon as Eric walked out into the street. As he approached the man, Eric spoke quietly.

"It's best if you walk away. Unless you feel like today is a good day to die."

"I won't be the one dying today."

"You that confident?"

"I'm faster than you."

"Well then… in that case… good luck." With that, Eric put some distance between himself and the man in the street. James had his hand on his pistol just in case the vagrant decided to try and shoot his brother in the back. Once he reached a decent distance, he turned around to face the man.

"Whenever you are ready, sir," Eric called out. And for a moment, the whole street was silent. The citizens watched in awe as they waited to see who would make the first move. The man tried to show strength and courage, but he could not hide his fear. Up until then, he had been certain he would win. But that certainty had all but vanished now as he stared down the street at the Desert Fox. Eric just stood there, steady as a rock. There was not a single trace of fear in his eyes. No fear and no doubt entered his mind. Just pure focus at the target before him. And the man knew that he could not back down now. As fast as he could, the man reached down for his pistol. But before it was completely out of its holster, Eric's bullet pierced his eye and tore through the back of his head. None of the citizens could believe the speed and accuracy that the Desert Fox just displayed. None that is except for his brother. They decided to spend the night there in the town and that night passed without incident. The following morning, Eric arose to a knock at his door. His immediate response was to pull his pistol and shoot a hole through the door. A voice responded immediately.

"Jesus Christ, Eric! I'm not a bad guy!" Kirk called out.

"You're also not six feet tall." Eric calmly responded. Kirk opened the door.

"Have you seen your brother?"

"No," Eric replied. "Why?"

Kirk went to the window and looked out.

"Someone's lookin' for him. A messenger of some kind." Eric rose and made his way to the window. Sure enough, a man was standing there in the street. He was wearing a long brown trench coat and a hat that covered most of his face. He turned his head slowly from side to side as he was looking around. Eric got dressed and made his way down to the street to confront the messenger.

"Can I help you?" Eric inquired.

"Are you James Harper?" the messenger asked.

"What do you want with him?"

"I have a message for him." the man replied. "The governor wants to meet with him."

"When?"

"As soon as possible." The man handed over a slip of paper.

"I'll see that he gets the message." With that, Eric turned and made his way back into the inn.

James returned a few minutes later and Eric delivered the message about the governor.

"I wonder what he wants," James asked himself out loud.

"Well, I'm comin' wit' you," Eric retorted.

"No, Eric. I need you to stay here with the others. I'll be back in the morning. See what you can find out about the gang."

"Understood." Eric relented. James gathered some stuff and left the inn and the town.

"Where he off to?" Bill asked Eric.

"To see the governor," Eric answered.

"The governor?" Bill came back with a bit of surprise. "What does he want?"

"Don't know."

When James arrived at the governor's office, he was politely escorted inside. He was led up a flight of stairs and through a set of huge and ornate red oak wooden doors. One man opened the door as another ushered James inside. As soon as he cleared the threshold of the doorway, the doors were closed behind him.

"Come in, Mr. Harper," came a pleasant and calm voice from a chair behind a desk. As the chair pivoted around, James took in his surroundings. It was a stunning room. There were beautiful oil paintings strategically placed around the walls. The fireplace was surrounded by an amazing hand-carved frame and mantle. The windows were covered with huge and thick curtains that looked like plush satin. The governor's desk was also ornately handcrafted. What he saw of the governor's chair, screamed comfort. And judging by the chair he was offered to sit in, it was a very loud scream. The governor was an older man with graying hair and a matching beard. He was moderately plump, but not too fat. The smile on his face showed he was at ease with himself. This helped James feel a little more relaxed about the situation. Although, he still did not know what was next.

"Hello, sir," James spoke up.

"Thank you for coming to see me," the governor responded.

"Thank you for the invite, sir." He was hoping that the rest of the meeting would be as pleasant and casual.

"You can go now, Jeffery," the governor said as he dismissed his aide. Jeffery made his way out of the room. When the governor and James were alone in the ornate setting, the meeting began.

"Now that we are alone, I have something to tell you. I know that you and a group of men have been riding around and killing off members of the Three Brothers Gang. And, in private I want to thank you for doing what should be done. However, I am the governor and I have to uphold the law."

"I know, sir," James said heavily.

"Which brings me to the reason I wanted to meet with you. It was the only way that I could inform you without countermanding the duties of this office."

"Inform me of what?" James inquired curiously and with a puzzled look on his face.

"That I will not be able to hold off the dogs for too much longer. I have been putting it off for as long as I could. You may only have a few more days before I have to intervene. Maybe a week at most. And you know what that means."

"Yes, sir. I do."

"Like I said, I believe you are doing the right thing. I do not want to intervene, but soon I will have no choice." The governor looked around calmly before turning his attention back to James. "Like I said… you have a few days, Mr. Harper. A week at most. I'm asking you to finish it before it is too late."

"Well, thank you for the heads-up, sir. I will do what I can as quickly as I can."

They said their goodbyes and James made his way out of the office. As he walked past the two men outside the door, they both smiled at him. James was not sure if they knew, but he returned the smile just the same.

On leaving the governor's office, James rode as hard and as fast as his poor horse could go. Soon after reaching the town where Eric and the others were waiting, James immediately requested a moment alone with his brother. The two men retreated to a secluded area.

"What do you suppose this is all about?" Chris asked as they moved away.

"Not sure," Bill responded. "But at least he wasn't arrested."

"That's a good sign," Kirk added. Then they heard the last part of the conversation as Eric spoke up.

"That's what we'll do then."

James and Eric made their way back to the others.

"It's almost over," James said. "We need to find one more man and quickly."

"To kill him?" Bill asked.

"To have him deliver a message," Eric answered. The group of men headed back over to the saloon.

"A message?" Kirk vocalized inquisitively. The other three did not understand. However, they followed James and Eric. They walked into the saloon and split off to speak to the patrons. It was a wild guess, but they got the answers they were looking for. Then, they went back to their rooms to gather the few belongings they carried. Eric went over to James' room.

"Whatcha doin'?" he asked. James handed over a piece of paper and then started writing again. Eric read the note aloud.

"As you may have noticed, my crew can go on and on picking your gang apart little by little. And I enjoy every minute of that. However, you and I both know a better way to end this. So… here is my solution. The five of us will be in Dry River Canyon to the south of the town. Meet us there at noon in two days and be prepared to end this finally. If you are not man enough, then we will continue to hunt your gang down and kill every last one of you. Oh, and make sure your father is there. I would really hate for him to miss this. Yours in death… the Desert Fox." Eric lowered the paper he had just finished reading. "Well, that is a cheerful salutation," he commented.

"I hope you don't mind. But I thought that was better than just James down."

"Works for me," Eric said tolerantly. Then he looked over and saw that James was still writing things down. As he finished and set the pen down, Eric inquired as to the nature of its contents.

"Oh, nothing. Just jotting some stuff down," James responded as he folded up the paper and placed it in his pocket. It was not long before they were on the trail again. With the information that they had acquired at the saloon mixed with Eric's ability to track people, they were soon on the member they were searching for. And when they found him, they made certain that he would deliver the message. And in a flash, the man was gone. The men made their way journey back to Dry River. When they passed on the outskirts of the last town they were just in, James asked them to wait. He then rode off alone and had returned in less than two hours.

"Okay" James stated on his return. "Let's get movin'."

"Everything okay, Jimmy?" Eric asked.

"Yep," James answered quickly. They pressed on and by nightfall before the second day, they were on the canyon. Dry River Canyon was small in the way canyons go. Its walls barely reached a hundred feet in the air and only about three hundred to four hundred feet wide at its apex. It was in its own right an extremely magnificent testimony to the beauty and the power of nature. The lining of the walls showing a glimpse of centuries past in striations of varying colors of brown and reddish hues. The river that had created this little wonder did not actually dry up. As can sometimes happen, the river moved underground and supplied water to the town just north of the canyon that bore its name. The men camped out at the top end of the canyon that night and had decided to head down into the canyon at first light to prepare for the oncoming battle. It was not long before Kirk and Chris and Bill were fast asleep. It seemed as though the coming day's event was nothing of a bother to them. James, however, sat up near the fire and occasionally looked up at the stars.

"What's on your mind?" Eric asked as he walked over to the fire and his brother.

"Can't sleep," James responded.

"I've had those days before."

"I just keep thinking of tomorrow," James said somberly. "Ever since we started this *crusade* all I could think about was the day it would finally be over."

"Believe me, Jimmy, I know." Eric consoled his brother with his words. "I've felt that way for a very long time. Even more so now that we are reunited."

"Yeah. I never thought that day would come in this life."

"That makes two of us."

"So… what do you think about our odds tomorrow?" James prodded his brother.

"Well, you can be sure that we will be outnumbered."

"That's a given."

"So, we need to make sure that we can get to cover quickly. Once there, we should have a better chance at picking them off."

"Agreed," James stated. After a pause, he followed up. "And I'm sure you can find that spot for us?"

"I'll check it out in the morning," Eric said calmly. "We should get some rest," he added. "Dawn will be here before we know it."

The two brothers left the fire and made their way to their makeshift beds. The night air was calm and peaceful. The lullaby of the crickets mixed with the crackling of the wood that was slowly being consumed by the dwindling yellow and orange flames was soothing. By morning, all that was left of the fire was a few thin wisps of smoke emanating from the smoldering remnants of the wood.

James arose just before daybreak. Everyone else was still asleep. Quietly, he hopped up onto his horse and rode off. It was not long after he disappeared that Eric's eyes greeted the pre-dawn. As he sat up, he noticed that James was gone as well as his horse. Eric paid no mind to his brother's disappearance, and he was soon on his own horse and on his way to scout the canyon. As he rode through the canyon, his eyes peered from side to side. Those eyes took in every detail of the canyon from the walls to the floor to any rock outcrop that could pose useful to increase their advantage over the obvious size of their enemy's group. It was about an hour or so before Eric returned to the camp. Bill and the others were now awake and apparently a little bothered by the initial waking up alone.

"What happened to you?" Bill asked calmly. Eric was climbing down from his horse as he answered the inquiry.

"I was surveying the canyon."

"Did you find anything useful?" Kirk questioned.

"Actually, yes. Yes, I did." Eric took up a stick and, in the loose and dry soil, drew a crude shape of the canyon. He then proceeded to show them where he felt the best spot was.

"Where the canyon is at its thinnest, there are several jutting rocks that we can quickly get to for cover when the shooting starts," Eric added. He detailed every move and every position where they should stand for their best chance. And the other question that was weighing on their minds was voiced.

"Where's James?" Kirk asked.

"We thought he was with you," Chris answered.

"No," Eric answered. "He left before I woke up."

"Do you think he's coming back?" Chris did not even mean to ask the question as he already knew the answer. But it came more from his own fear rather than that of anyone else. And his lips moved before he could catch himself.

Hey!" Eric snapped back as he drew his pistol and pointed it straight at Chris. "My brother is *no* coward!

If you ever make a reference like that again, I'll drop you before you say the last word of that sentence."

It was clear that everyone was on edge this morning. In a way, which was a good thing. It would help to keep them sharp and alert. Chris apologized quickly and Eric lowered his arm. A horse appeared in the distance. As it got closer, they all recognized the rider. It was James.

"Out for a morning ride, Jimmy?" Eric casually asked as James's horse clip-clopped into camp.

"I was sightseeing," James responded. "Dave and his men are about two miles out. Northward."

"How many?" Bill asked.

"About twenty to twenty—five men," James answered. A solemn and grave look befell Bill and Chris and Kirk. James looked back to his brother. "Did you find anything in the canyon that could help us?"

"Well... we are outnumbered at least four to one if not five to one," Eric responded. "But there is a spot that will give us a small tactical advantage."

Eric outlined his plan for his brother. The others, who had already seen this outline, watched again.

"I hope it's enough," James added at the end of the run-through.

"One way or the other it will be," Eric replied. "It has to be because it's the best we got."

They packed up their camp and gathered their weapons. All the rifles and pistols were loaded fully, and the remaining ammo was stashed in quick and easily accessible locations. Leaving the horses tied up, they ventured down into the canyon. They had reached the spot that Eric had detailed in the plan. James looked around. It was better than he saw it in his mind during the explanation of the area.

"This will actually do quite nicely," James remarked. "We shouldn't have too much trouble."

There was no fear in his voice.

"How can you be so nonchalant?" Chris asked with a hint of irritation laced in his voice due to James's apparent lack of concern about the present situation. "We are outnumbered five to one, and you're treating it as if it were some kind of duck hunt!"

"Because I know that good always wins against evil in the end. Besides, I'm counting on them to make a fatal mistake," James responded calmly.

"And what mistake would that be?" Bill chimed in.

"Miscalculation," James answered. As his voice trailed off, the hooves of several horses could be heard in the distance. It almost sounded like a stampede as the sound reverberated throughout the canyon.

"Everyone, take up your place," Eric ordered. Within seconds, everyone was in his spot and ready for the ultimate battle. It was not long before the sound of those horses turned into flesh and bone as Dave and the rest of the Three Brothers Gang appeared. They slowed their horses when they reached the single row of five men who were anxiously awaiting their arrival. David and his father climbed down from the perches of their saddles and made their way to James and Eric. David looked up towards the sun for a moment. As he turned his focus back towards the men before him his voice opened up.

"Today looks like a great day to die, don't it?" David remarked casually.

James paused for a moment and turned his head upward. He glared for a moment at the crystal blue sky and the only star visible that was nearing the apex of its journey for the day.

"Indeed, it is," James confirmed. Then, with a slight nod of the head, he continued, "Unless you wish to surrender to us now."

David let out a hearty laugh as he looked behind himself at the group of men behind him and then back to the minute number of men before him.

"Us…? Surrender to you?!" David said incredulously, his eyes mocking.

"Yes," James retorted without flinching even the slightest. "It's not too late," he added. David's eyes returned a scowl at James. His eyes would set James on fire if that were possible.

"I've got twenty—five men…!" David stated with irritable aggression. Eric looked to his brother and then back at David as he started to speak. Without a thought, Eric cut him off.

"Five to one," he stated firmly.

David started over.

"I got twenty—five men behind me! Against your what... five!? And you think I would surrender to *you*!?" David exclaimed in a voice full of insult.

"Absolutely," James said at once. His body remained calm, and he still showed no signs of fear at the large group of men before him. Three of the other four men that stood with him had no clue how he could remain so calm. And even though Eric knew how this could be, he was still immensely impressed with his brother's courage and composure.

"You got some set of balls, kid." David's father spoke out. "But it will be a cold day in hell before we would ever surrender to you."

"Last chance, David," James said softly, cocking his head slightly to the side as he spoke. As he finished, the sound of about fifty rifles could be heard cocking and being prepped to fire. David looked up as did everyone else. Everyone else except for James who kept his gaze solely on David. On the rim of the canyon on either side stood about fifty men from the infantry. Their sights were trained on David and his men. It was at this moment that Eric and the others put two and two together. Back in the other town, James was writing a second letter. And when he rode off into the night alone, he dispatched that letter to its intended reader. The message that read:

"You will be pleased to know that in two days, everything will be over. Also, it would be fair to note that the Three Brothers Gang will be in Dry River

Canyon where they are plotting to attack the nearby town and murder its sheriff. As I am the sheriff of this town, I would appreciate any help you can give pertaining to the safety of my town and my own life.

Your Obedient Servant:

James Harper"

was soon perused by the governor. Because of the way the letter was transcribed, the governor could legally justify getting involved. He dispatched fifty men from the infantry with whom James had met up with earlier that morning. He had explained to them what to do and when. Back in the canyon, Eric was even more impressed with his brother's ingenuity. David knew that there was no way out of this one. If they tried to run, they would be shot down without any hesitation. He knew that there was no way that they could surrender and face a judge who would certainly hang every last one of them. David also knew that his men were loyal and would fight to the death if so ordered. And with the three options, that was the best one he felt was available. Without any further hold and recourse, he shouted out to his men.

"TO HELL BOYS!"

At that moment everyone scattered like roaches when the lights come on. James' men knew the terrain and quickly took up their spots while the members of the Three Brothers Gang scrambled frantically to find cover from the hail of bullets that rained down over them. Four of them were killed in that first round along with two of their horses. But the majority of them made it to cover including David and his father. At that point, it really became a fair fight. The infantry had trouble getting clear shots and they also had very little cover except for laying down on the rim of the canyon. While the main objective was to kill James and Eric and the others, some had to take on the militia above. It seemed, at least at the moment, that the only ones to fall were some of the infantrymen. The canyon provided better cover than expected for both sides of the men inside the canyon. As bullets decimated the rocks above Eric and James' heads, they returned fire. James managed to pick off another gang member.

"I see your aim has gotten better, Jimmy," Eric said jovially.

"Or maybe yours has gotten worse," James retorted in a similar tone. Some of the infantry shifted their position and from their new vantage point took out five more members of the gang. The other members moved to counter the change and took up safe cover. One of them, while moving, squeezed off a round that struck Eric. He fell back from the shot and looked down.

"You, okay?" James asked. He was concerned but did not move his gaze from the gang members. Eric looked down at the blood coming from his left shoulder and then back to his brother.

"Yeah. It's not that bad," he replied. And it really was not. The bullet only grazed his shoulder. Chris stood up to shoot another man who was running, but a bullet pierced his right leg and he dropped to the ground and scooted back to cover. He took his bandana from his pocket and tied it just above the wound.

"Man, that hurts," Chris stated trying to make light of it.

"Well, then next time keep your ass down," Kirk responded with a smile. And within moments the two of them were back in the fight. Eric, even with his left arm partially out of commission from the grazing of a bullet, kept up the firing and took out two more members of the gang. The fighting never died down and neither side was willing to yield.

"Man..." James said with a smile, "when are these boys gonna give up?"

"I don't know!" Eric bantered back. "Why don't you ask them?"

"I don't think they can hear me." James stood up for a moment and took aim. With the squeeze of the trigger, another gang member fell. "It's too noisy down here," he added.

The militia changed positions once again and in doing so, found a way to take out a few more members of the gang. After a few more missed shots, James fired once more. This time, his bullet struck the target he had missed twenty-five years ago. David's father fell back in death as David screamed, "FATHER!" But there was no hope for his father. The man was dead before his body even hit the ground. David grabbed his father's pistol and in pure anger and rage, he wielded both pistols and rose to his feet. With no fear of recourse, he started firing blindly in the direction of his assailants. Three bullets struck his body and David fell back and landed near his father's body. He was mortally wounded but he was still alive. The militia, along with James and Eric and the others, took out the rest of the members of the Three Brother's Gang. When it was over and the last member had fallen, James and Eric made their way over to David who lay there in immense pain and bleeding profusely. They quickly took up the two pistols that were near him and tossed them far to the side.

"Think we should put him out of his misery?" James calmly asked his brother.

"No…" Eric answered. "Let the bastard suffer. He'll die soon enough."

They turned their backs and started walking over to the other men. What they did not count on was that David had one last trick up his sleeve. That trick was a small Derringer pistol. James heard the click of the hammer and instinctively turned to get between Eric and David. As he made this move, James shouted out, "NO!" just as the shot was fired from David's little devil. The bullet ripped through James' torso. The damage was fatal. Eric pulled his pistol and sent that man straight to hell with one shot right between the eyes. James fell into his brother, who laid him gently on the ground. Eric cradled his brother. As he assessed the situation, he knew that nothing could be done.

"You were right," James said softly through the pain within his body. "I would give my life for you."

And although Eric knew that his brother was soon to join his parents, he tried to still give hope.

"Nah…" he said, trying to be calm, "you'll make it. I've seen worse."

In truth, it took everything Eric had not to break down. Bill and Chris and Kirk were now standing over the two brothers, but none of them spoke. James took out his father's pistol. Laying it on his chest, he spoke once again.

"Keep 'em together."

"I will," Eric replied as he was still fighting every urge to cry.

"Eric…" James said roughly as his breathing grew shorter. "Pl… ease … ta… ke care o… of… mah… fa… il… y." His words were broken up with rasping breaths and coughs.

"I promise."

Life had all but left his brother alone.

"One… m… more th… ing."

"Anything."

"Ta… take… me… take me ho… home."

This plea was the last words anyone would ever hear from him. The final long breath escaped his lungs as they deflated for the last time. James' body slumped limply in his brother's arms. And for the first time in twenty-five years, Eric's eyes welled up heavily with tears. He would have done anything to have traded places with his brother. But he knew that this was impossible. He also knew what he must do. And it was the one thing that he had hoped not to have to do when this all began. The commander and two members of the infantry hitched up a small flatbed wagon and they helped Eric hoist his brother's body up onto the back of it. Then, ten of the infantry, and the commander, accompanied Eric and Bill and the others to Dry River. As they entered the town, the citizens noticed the procession. The street began to fill up as they watched their beloved sheriff's body being pulled through on the makeshift hearse of the day. Someone ran ahead of the gathering to tell Katherine of the procession. Sarah was sleeping as Katherine emerged from the house. As she looked on, she noticed Eric. She then saw Kirk and Bill and Chris along with the members of the infantry. And finally, she noticed the horse-drawn flatbed carriage that carried all of her hopes and dreams. The one who had all her love lay motionless within. Tears poured from her eyes as she ran to the wagon. Standing there beside it, she looked over the edge and down on her husband. Deep within her heart, she was hoping that he was asleep and would soon rise. But her mind let her see the painful reality of what lay before her. The commander walked over to her side. And although he knew that no words could ever truly offer any comfort, he spoke up.

"You should know that your husband was a very brave man. He will receive the highest honor from the governor."

Through choking tears, she thanked him slowly.

Eric, who was standing next to Katherine spoke solemnly.

"He gave his life to save mine," he said, looking over the edge at his brother. In the back of her mind, she expected to hear as much. For that was his nature. It was who he was. It was what he did.

The following day, Eric and Katherine and Bill and the others went to fulfil the first promise that Eric made to his brother. And as they emerged from the trees to the clearing, they could see a vacant cottage that showed the signs of ages of abandonment. The once well— maintained abode was all but unrecognizable. Nature had spent the last twenty—five years reclaiming the land. Certain wildlife had made it their home. The body that was left on the porch had long since been picked apart and carried off by hungry scavengers. To everyone else, the desolation before them was not so much out of the ordinary. But to Eric, it was immensely saddening. As he looked at the place that he once called home, he could see in his mind how it used to be. The front door swung open as two boys ran out holding cane poles. In the doorway stood his mother, just as he had remembered her. The smile she gave brought a slight one to Eric's face. Then, as he looked to the side of the house, he could see his father standing there showing the two boys how to hold a pistol. His eyes could see all of this as if it were real. As Eric continued to look around, he noticed the three wooden crosses that his brother had fashioned from branches to mark the remains of his mother and his father and the empty plot that was thought to be for him. Somehow, they managed to remain in place. Slowly, he led the horse-drawn carriage up to where the crosses stood. The men each took up a shovel and started to dig up the third mound. They made the hole much deeper than the other two. Once it was dug, they planted the shovels into the fresh mound of dirt beside the excavated gravesite. With very heavy hearts, they lifted the pine box from the carriage that contained the body of a beloved brother and husband and father. Carefully, they lowered the coffin into the hole. In a slow and somber movement, they covered the pine box with the dirt. When they had finished, Bill gathered up the shovels and returned them to the back of the wagon. Eric stood over his brother's grave. Katherine was holding Sarah and was standing beside him. After they had silently said their goodbyes, Katherine had reached down and taken up Eric's hand with a gentle squeeze. Then she led Sarah back to the front of the wagon. Eric dropped his head and then walked over to stand between the graves of his mother and father. He knelt down and placed a hand on each of the two grassy mounds. He closed his eyes and once again lowered his head. Quietly, in his heart and in his mind, he finally said farewell to them. When the moment had passed, he rose to his feet and slowly made his way back to his horse. As he put a foot into his stirrup, he paused and looked back at the three wooden crosses.

"You're finally home, Jimmy," he quietly whispered. He then pulled himself up into the saddle and turned his horse around. Soon they were on their way back to Dry River. Just before they left the clearing, Eric turned back one last time. Although he did not say goodbye, it was clearly visible all across his face and definitely within his eyes. At that moment a soft and gentle breeze arose and lightly lifted his hair. In his heart, he knew it was from James. A smile came across his face once again and his voice echoed out.

"Hee-yah!" His horse took off and the cottage disappeared. Eric kept his other promise to his brother as well. Two years after the battle of Dry River Canyon and the death of his brother, Sarah was a precious little three—year—old running through the yard. Eric stood there watching in pride. He could see so much of James in her. Around his waist was the belt that once graced his father's side and then his only brother's. And within the holsters were the two hand-carved ivory inlaid handled pistols. They were together once more. On Eric's lapel was the silver starred badge, that symbol of authority that said, 'Sheriff — Dry River'. Katherine stood by his side watching her little girl. She was radiant as ever before although in her heart she still missed the man she loved. She had a little boy of about one year in her arm. This little boy was the spitting image of his father. Rachel then appeared alongside Katherine. She reached out for the little boy.

"Mommy's here," she said.

Eric kept his promise. He and Rachel had married just over a year before. They settled down in Dry River and together they were by her side and helping Katherine and Sarah. And in honor of the two greatest men he would ever know, Eric gave his son the only name he could.

John James.

www.ingramcontent.com/pod-product-compliance
Lightning Source LLC
LaVergne TN
LVHW091557060526
838200LV00036B/876